The New Lone Ranger

by

Rex Marlin

RoseDog Books
PITTSBURGH, PENNSYLVANIA 15238

RoseDog Books
585 Alpha Drive
Suite 103
Pittsburgh, PA 15238
Visit our website at *www.rosedogbookstore.com*

ISBN: 978-1-4809-7636-8
eISBN: 978-1-4809-7659-7

The New Lone Ranger

"If there's nothing more important to a man than his relationship with Christ, can a Christian man survive in a Non-Christian environment?"

—Rex Marlin

Chapter One

He arrived in town sometime in March of 1983 on a Greyhound Bus. The town was Chicago. The Windy City. The Hog Butcher. Where this unmasked man came from was only known to him. He called himself Robin McElroy. What his real name was, nobody really knows. The Chicago night air was loaded with smog in a dismal inky sky which shrouded the white stars. Elderly streetlights glowed with a hazy sheen surrounding them in the cool night air. The drone of automobile engines, the racket of truck and bus motors permeated the air. Noise pollution. There was an icy breeze blowing off of Lake Michigan which was within walking distance of this particular vicinity. When Robin looked up to a street sign which loomed on a street corner, it read: *Halsted Street.*

This mysterious figure was clad in a black leather jacket, shiny ebony-colored cowboy boots, faded blue jeans, a vermillion-colored sweatshirt, a chocolate-colored belt with a Winchester Rifle etched in the buckle, and, most profound amongst his apparel was a long, gold necklace which suspended a large shining cross from it. What did he look like? He had medium-length blond hair, parted in the middle, but not recently cut. Robin, as he called himself, had the most captivating blue eyes which were filled with wonder. His cheekbones were set high, a Roman Nose indicated strong character, and his lips were a thin red line. His build was mesomorph. He weighed about 170 pounds. He walked like a cat.

This man just drifted into town with no kin to account for. When somebody looked at him, an air of reticence was the first thing to be detected. He seemed to wish for people to keep their distance from him, and he, in turn, would keep his distance from them. Robin McElroy was somewhat of a "spirit." He was present, either the center of attention or in the background, yet reticent from all around him. There was no way this Christian Man was going to be swayed in his ways by society's toxicity.

The Saint James Hotel was teeming with patrons during the 1930s when it first opened. This seven-story red brick structure had deteriorated with age. The red bricks were now a brownish-red. Soot from thousands of days in Chicago's polluted air had taken its toll on the structure. There were a couple of broken windows to be seen from the front. Out front attached to the building was a big yellow neon sign that protruded towards the street reading in dulled red letters: The Saint James Hotel. The neon sign had a couple of holes in it where the white light inside shone through it. Tacky. The entrance-way was right under the neon sign. It was a black painted door, the old-fashioned kind, made of wood with an antique door handle. This sight came into view while Robin McElroy strolled along the sidewalk parallel to Halsted Street and a city park called Manteno Park. The New Lone Ranger, as he may have been thought to be, drew in closer to this hotel.

Robin McElroy was toting a large suitcase and a small suitcase. The small suitcase had a combination lock on it. Inside, the small suitcase was loaded with bills bearing the portrait of Ulysses S. Grant. Where all that may came from, the fact being Mr. McElroy hadn't worked in over the past three years, was unknown. As a matter of fact, nobody but the man carrying that bag knew what was in it. The other suitcase, of course, contained his clothing and a few personal items. One other item he was toting in the same hand as the small suitcase was an AM/FM radio.

Right now he was ambulating at a rapid cadence along a sidewalk which passed through Manteno Park. Halsted Street was to the back of him now. A car horn cut the night air. It was an impatient taxi driver in a yellow checker cab attempting to speed up the time he was arriving at his destination. In the outdoors, the clacking of his cleats on the heels of his boots could be heard on the sidewalk. There was a foul smell in all the air around him. It was sulfur, or something. Industrial waste, belched from the smokestack of manufacturing firms in operation twenty-four hours a day. Robin looked up at the somewhat captivating sign which read *The Saint James Hotel* one more time before crossing a street. He had reached the end of Manteno Park. He was now located on Manteno Park's North Side. McElroy walked across the street, then put his large suitcase down to open the weather-beaten front door. After opening the door, he disappeared inside.

Inside, there was a dark alcove and, around a bend, the registration desk. The desk now had a steel screen painted gray and lined with rust between the desk clerk and the customer. The customer had to slide his money through a beaten metal drawer, then the desk clerk would slide the key back through that drawer. The rates were posted next to the screen on a white wooden sign in red letters: $8.15 a night. S45 a week. $155 a month. Cheap.

An obese, scar-faced, cigar-smoking desk clerk appeared at the screen and noted Robin looking over the room-rates sign. He watched him for a moment, then met the customer eye to eye.

"What'll it be?" the desk clerk asked him in a guttural voice. There was an immediate no-nonsense tone in his voice and the way he looked at someone.

"One month," McElroy replied.

The desk clerk reached for a slip of paper to pass through the beaten drawer to the hotel patron.

"I'll need to see your driver's license," the desk clerk added. "No credit cards or checks are accepted."

McElroy removed his wallet from his blue jean's pocket. He had a false driver's license bearing the name and personal information for a fictitious character named Robin McElroy. He displayed this phony credential through the screen to the seedy desk clerk. The big man looked it over and filled in some of the information from it on the slip of paper. When he was finished scribbling some of that information down, he passed the slip of paper through the beaten metal drawer and told Robin.

"I'll need your signature and one hundred and fifty-five clams. Is there anybody with you?"

"No." Robin Mc Elroy replied.

There was a black ballpoint pen tied to a string under the white sign posting the room rates. After Robin scribbled down his John Hancock at the bottom of the slip of paper, he reached into his wallet and with the form slid three fifty-dollar bills and a "sawbuck" into the drawer. The desk clerk looked over what he had delivered to him skeptically, then removed his big brown cigar from the ash tray, took a puff, and returned it to the ash tray. The foul odor of cigar smoke escaped his fat lips and wafted through the rusted gray screen. To Robin McElroy, the cigar smoke was like a punch in the nose.

"I don't want any police up here," the desk clerk told McElroy firmly. "If I see them up here just once because of you, you're out!"

The New Lone Ranger nodded in approval while the desk clerk slid his key with a black tag in gold letters which said: "23" on it through the drawer. Robin knew better than to ask if there was a housekeeping service. Instead of telling Robin where his room was, the obese desk clerk disappeared back into his room after scooping his cigar out of his ash tray. Twenty-three Robin, thought. That should be simple enough. It's the third room on the second floor. There was a dark and eerie staircase to the left of McElroy from the front desk. He followed that gloomy passageway to the second floor.

When he arrived at the black wooden door that read "23" in white painted letters on it, he put his bags down and unlocked the rattletrap lock. The door, on the second floor of the hotel, as he had predicted, creaked when it opened.

He flicked the light switch beside the door, which clicked a loud "click" when he did, and a twenty-five-watt bulb dangling from a cord cast its illumination over the dismal hotel room.

To Robin's immediate right side in the bedroom was a scratched and scarred brown wooden chest of drawers, no doubt installed when the hotel first opened. Above it, an oval-shaped mirror with a dark brown wooden frame had its share of nicks in it. There was a slight cloudiness covering the glass in the mirror. At least it wasn't cracked. Atop the chest of drawers and to the side of the oval mirror was a lamp that's drabness reeked of the plainness so common in 1950s technocracy. The lamp's base was painted a dull hue of black; the shade was a gloomy gray. Robin twisted the tiny black switch on it and a soft light projected through the shade, illuminating a mish-mash of spiral designs scrawled around it.

The yellow and white striped wallpaper in the room was faded, dog-eared at the corners. The alarums of nicks in the wooden floorboards had been painted over with black enamel. Ten feet across the room was a mattress on a somewhat rusted steel frame; no sheets were included. The closet on the west side of the room was an open affair with three hangers suspended from a metal pipe which stretched across the upper portion.

To his right, in the southwest corner were the bathroom quarters. It was a squared-off portion in the bedroom which jutted inward, designated by two walls and a door. The black wooden door to the bathroom had been left open, and Robin could see the white porcelain toilet from the doorway of his bedroom. McElroy stuck a cigarette in his mouth and walked across the wooden floorboards. He peered into the bathroom, then switched on the light in it. The light in the bathroom was another twenty-five-watt bulb dangling from a cord in the center of the ceiling. When its light was cast throughout the bathroom quarters, the first thing to catch his eye was the white porcelain sink trough. The porcelain in the sink trough was stained with a wide line of brown rust originating at the faucet. Two lesser lines of rust streaked the trough below the hot and cold water knobs. The chrome on the faucet and hot and cold water knobs had worn off and what was left was flat gray steel lined with rust. The toilet was brown below the water-line where the porcelain enamel had worn off. The chrome flush-lever hung loose, most likely requiring jostling to make it work. The bathtub was a big, deep basin resting on the floor, with rust around the drain and also streaked below the faucet and hot and cold water knobs. Two of the white, gold-speckled tiles on the bathroom floor were chipped. The tiles had no wax or polish left on them.

Robin passed through the bathroom door and returned to his bedroom. He stood in the middle of his room and looked the whole thing over one more time. So this was it!

"Perfect," he mumbled to himself. For $55 a month, could he really ask for anything more?

He removed a steel lighter from the inside pocket on his black leather jacket which was still covering his back. He ignited the cigarette which had been left hanging from between his lips. His baggage was still set out in the hallway outside his door. He stepped across the nicked black wooden floorboards and rustled up the large suitcase, the small suitcase, and the AM/FM radio. He closed the bedroom door, then twisted his room key in the hole just below the doorknob to lock it. His luggage remained just inside the doorway to his room. He lifted the two suitcases with both hands and transported the luggage to his open closet, placing them inside of it.

There was a window next to his bed. There were no curtains around the window; just a tattered off-white window shade that had been drawn all the way down. Robin knelt down upon his mattress and tugged on the white plastic loop below the shade. The shade sprang all the way up to the top of the window in a flash! Cheap. The street he lived on, its name still unknown to him, and Manteno Park could be seen outside of his window. They were in plain view amongst the streetlights. Halsted Street could be seen in the distance with its constant flow of traffic traveling upon it. The traffic on Halsted Street was relatively light at this late hour in the night. To Robin's immediate left, he could see the illuminated sign that read "The Saint James Hotel."

McElroy switched on his portable radio and adjusted the tuning dial on FM band. A song that sounded good to him was detected on the 96th frequency. He lay back on his mattress, still puffing on the cigarette he'd lighted a minute ago. It was relatively quiet at this hour in the hotel. No doubt, he thought, everybody else is in bed. The time on his Timex wristwatch read 2:27. Robin was finally beginning to tire. It had been a long ride on that Greyhound Bus. He often fell asleep while listening to his prized radio.

"This is The Windy City's Big 96, 96 on your FM dial. Robert Farley here with you until six o'clock. The Big 96 has more rock and talk than all the rest of them, so why don't you keep your fingers off of that button and stay tuned in to us? Here's a golden oldie from the year of 1965: 'Tired of Waitin' For You,' by the Kinks."

Robin remembered that song from when he was a boy. That song came at the time when the British Invasion for music into the United States was in full swing. Groups from England such as: The Beatles, Herman's Hermits, Gerry and the Pacemakers, Freddie and the Dreamers, The Dave Clark Five, The Kinks, Peter and Gordon, The Rolling Stones and many many more dominated the American charts with music from Great Britain. While that song was playing over his black Panasonic unit, he held the cross on his necklace between his fingers and stared at it. This symbol meant so much to him. This cross necklace meant more to him than anything else he had ever owned. While he continued to gaze upon the shiny cross clamped between his fingers, he said to it, "So tired."

Chapter Two

To look at Robin McElroy one would say he was about twenty-five years old. Actually, he was eight years older than that. His youth was gone. Robin was now a man of the world. Terminal youth? Maybe that was true in some men. Maybe it was true in many men. Anybody who thought The New Lone Ranger was still wet behind the ears was believing balderdash. What was his goal in life now? Did he have one? He ought to have a goal in life at the late age of thirty-three years. But he didn't. He just took every day as it came and was biding his time to join Jesus. He had no fixed direction or goal or plan for his remaining days on this earth. He was free, just like a seagull flying over the sea with no definite plans but to live for today.

When he awoke the following morning, he immediately looked out the window; he'd left the shade all the way up the night before. The skies outside were gray. A light rain was falling upon the street below his window. The rain was mixed with snow. When he turned to his right while lying upon that concoction of a bed he'd slept on, he noticed an old fashioned black-colored heating unit standing three feet tall against the wall opposite the closet. It was the east wall of the room, close to the bedroom door. The door was actually on the northeast corner of the room, located on the north wall. He'd missed that heating unit the night before. After rolling off the bed, he walked two steps and touched the top of the metal unit. It was a dull shade of ebony. Hot! Good, he thought. At least the heat works in this joint.

Robin ambulated into the bathroom. He was only wearing his briefs at this time. There were no towels in the john, or even a place to hang one!

Great! A couple of towels would be the first thing on his shopping list that day. In the meantime, he removed a black comb from the pocket of his blue jeans which he'd recklessly tossed beside his bed before retiring the night before. His cross necklace still hung from his neck, the cross on it was suspended between two nipples on a background of hair. There was the stubble of a beard on his face; he rubbed it with his fingers, noting he required a shave. There was an electric razor in his large suitcase; and thank God for the electrical outlet beside the bathroom mirror above the sink.

While that electric razor was buzzing away the stubble on his face, Robin reminisced about something his mother had told him. He could see her standing there in the kitchen of his home in Kansas. She was a white-haired woman with a wizen suntanned face and a slim build. She was wearing a white dress with flowers on it.

"The amount of work you do around here could be put in a thimble."

There was an ever-present firmness in her voice. Degradation. That's what Robin thought it was. She was only trying to belittle her son. That's how he interpreted it.

"Right, Ma." he whispered quietly while leaving the old kitchen.

It seemed to him that during his entire life he'd been persecuted. Degraded. Everybody was trying to strip Robin McElroy of his pride. Now, today, reflecting back to his hotel room in The St. James Hotel, he was "alone" and "safe."

Another figment of his life surfaced in his mind's eye. Robin was a teenager standing at the loading dock of a firm he once had worked for. His pay was peanuts. Penny-ante. His boss was a slender man with kinky gray hair, black bushy eyebrows, and a suntanned face. The older man was looking down at this young lad from atop the dock. Robin was standing in the cement area where the trucks dipped in.

"You're a nice guy," his boss was telling him. "I hate to do this, but I have to let you go. Your work has just not measured up to what I expect of my boys on the loading dock. Would you like me to write up your last paycheck now, or would you like to have it mailed to you?"

In retrospect, Robin thought, taking his buzzing razor off of his face in the mirror of The St. James Hotel, that was bullshit! Robin McElroy was an excellent worker. He always had been an excellent worker. The reality of the whole thing was just that he didn't fit.

Robin's train of thought jumped to a sudden halt. He rubbed his face with his fingers. His countenance was now smoothed of the stubble. He walked back into the bedroom and removed a toothbrush and toothpaste from his large suitcase, then returned to the bathroom quarters. While brushing his teeth, he began to think again.

A woman with long dark brown hair, parted on the side with a barrette in it was talking to Robin. She had a neatly chiseled, foxy face with deep-set green eyes and a tall, slender build. "I'll always love you," Mary LaTella, an old girlfriend, once told him. "I'll always love you," she repeated.

Mary LaTella was a tall and slender brunette whom Robin had once been very much in love with. He could see her standing there in the sand of his hometown beach wearing her yellow bikini. She had a deep brown suntan. He'd remained her friend for many years, and gave Mary credit for "sculpturing" this man he now was. He'd first met Miss LaTella in high school. It evolved into a post-high school relationship. He had never asked her to marry him, but for about one year he had wanted to. The visitation between the two of them had never become frequent enough to warrant a proposal. During those youthful days he dreamed and dreamed. He dreamed he would still be breathing her shit when her hair was gray. Her "box" was catnip and he was a cat. He wanted to plant his nose in her "tuna boat" all night and dream of the ocean. Was that all he saw in her? No. Not really. There was more to Mary LaTella than just that. To Robin McElroy, Mary LaTella was the epitome of a woman. The pinnacle of womanhood. And at the mere age of twenty, she seemed to have the wisdom of a forty-year-old. Unique. Special.

With Mary, Robin could see the sunshine on a cloudy day. She was pure and, to him, immortal. Why she left him, he could never understand. All of Mary was behind him now. She had gone off and married another man. Had he waited too long to ask? Had he not been aggressive enough with her? To him, there was still no way of knowing.

Mary had taken this rough-edged ladies' man and cultivated him, honed him down into someone who was really something. So he thought. She'd taken all that time to bake that cake, then she left that cake out in the rain to ruin. But that cake didn't ruin. Instead, it endured.

"If you dream of screwing me," she told Robin, "through the eyes of God, it's just as bad as doing it. Thinking of or planning to do something wrong in God's eyes is just as bad as going through with doing it."

Mary LaTella was religious and had a great influence in that respect with McElroy too.

Robin gazed back down upon that big, gold cross that was suspended between his nipples. Mary had given him that cross for Christmas one year. There was no possession of Robin's he valued more than that cross.

Nobody else could have that cross. Nobody.

He twisted on the hot water knob on the sink and waited for it to heat up. He twisted on a little bit of the cold water too. When the water was just the right temperature inside of the trough, he put the open palms of his hands under the water and splashed the water on his face. In a few seconds, his face and hands were dripping wet. He knew he had no towel to dry them off. He entered his bedroom and used a sweatshirt to dry them off.

"Why didn't I ask her to marry me?" he asked himself. "There will never be another anything like her. Mary LaTella can never be replaced. I am what I am thanks to her."

Did The New Lone Ranger really want to get married? Well? Maybe. But it certainly couldn't be to just any Jane, Sally, or Mary.

Chapter Three

Robin slipped on a blue sweat shirt. It was still raining outdoors. He watched a car go by on the street below his hotel room window. Manteno Park, to the south of him, was void of people on this cold, late winter day. The snow, which was still falling out of the skies mixed with the rain, was not sticking. The grass in the park was brown and dead. There was still an accumulation of leaves in some places from the previous autumn. Trees in the park were all naked of leaves. Spring, though, was just around the corner. And life goes on, he thought to himself.

McElroy returned to the bathroom and ran his black comb through his hair. Robin was careful to make the part down the middle straight. His mother had always taught her son to be tidy. Neat as pin. She was as neat as a pin. This time the cake in the rain did not endure to quite the same degree. There were days when Robin failed to shave, period. There were days when he didn't comb his hair until almost noon. Oftentimes he only brushed his teeth once a day instead of three times a day. He combed his blond hair back along the sides.

He looked over what he was doing to it in the mirror. He stared at his countenance from angle, then shifted his stance and gazed at his visage from yet another. Robin cast a tough, yet somewhat "pouty" look into the bathroom mirror.

"Elvis," he said to himself in a deep, Southern voice.

McElroy looked over his hair some more. It looked good to him now, but he reckoned it needed to be cut. A haircut would be on the agenda in due time. His time.

Back in his bedroom, the fifty-year-old chest of drawers beside his door had five levels of drawers. He slid open the bottom one and placed his small suitcase inside of it. There were two glass diamond-shaped knobs on each drawer to be held when opening and closing them.

Lazily, he plopped back atop his mattress and removed a cigarette and the steel lighter from the inside pocket of his black leather jacket which was a crumpled heap on the floor beside his bed. He flicked the flint on the lighter and a yellow flame with a blue base at the wick appeared. He placed the flame against the tip of his cigarette and took a drag off of it. The tip of the cigarette glowed orange, and a grayish-white plume of smoke escaped his lips and the end of the cigarette, rising gently in the still air of his bedroom.

Robin switched on the radio beside his bed. It was resting on the black enamel floor. The song "We've Got Tonight," by Kenny Rogers and Sheena Easton, was playing on this predominantly contemporary radio station, Chicago's Big 96. When the song came to an end, there was a quick moment of silence, then a disc-jockey's voice popped on over the air. This time, the voice was female.

"Here's fantastic news from the friendly people at Klondike! Now is the time of year for Klondike's 50 percent off sale. Our valued customers should know this 50 percent off sale is an annual event at Klondike.

"Yes! Or half price you can have a rug cleaned.

"If you wish, you can have two rooms of carpeting cleaned for the usual cost of just one. That upholstered sofa and chair you need to have cleaned can be done for half price if you do it this week.

"The Klondike quality and service during this sale is just as professional as ever. No corners are cut. The only difference is that the price is cut in half! Drop by or call Klondike for the amazing details.

"Klondike is always busy during this sale. We don't want to let anybody down. Get your call in today at 466-3737. That's 466-3737, Suburbs, see your phone book. VISA and Master Charge are welcome. Give us a call today.

"Jenny Bright here with you on Chicago's Big 96. WZMX. Accuweather. Get out your raincoat! It's going to be raining all day, mixed with a light amount of snow. I'm ready for spring. Are you? We're looking at a high of 36, a low of 18 tonight, with no wind chill. That's right, no wind chill factor today. Presently I've got thirty-one at O'Hare, 32 at the Lakefront and 32 at WZMX. The time is 10:37.

"It's hot this week, here's 'Do You Really Want to Hurt Me?' by Culture Club at The Big 96…."

There was some noise coming from the room next door and to the east of him. A man and a woman were arguing. They were ranting and raving. What could possibly be so bad between the two of them, Robin thought, that would cause them to carry on in such a juvenile manner? To him, they sounded just like two little kids fighting over a cherished bag of candy. It was ridiculous. Seeing that the wall between them was solid plaster, it muffled their voices enough so what they were yelling at each other about could not be construed. Nonetheless, the "drone" of their spiteful conversation was invading McElroy's ears. Robin turned the volume up on his radio, and "Do You Really Want to Hurt Me?" squelched out the agitated behavior coming from the couple next door.

Robin surmised it was going to be a long, boring day.

Chapter Four

Rubin Paccino's Italian Café was just two short blocks away from The Saint James Hotel. It was an orange brick building with long rectangular windows surrounding the outer portion from all sides. The roof was black shingles on a forty-five degree angle with an orange-colored ornament on top of it in the middle. Rubin Paccino's appeared to have been built within the past twenty years according to the structural design it displayed.

On that very same morning, Robin ventured that establishment with a growling sensation in the pit of his stomach. He hadn't eaten in more than a day. He was starving! He seated himself at a chrome swivel chair with a padded orange-colored top on it at the counter of the cafe. He took immediate notice of the breakfast menu set on the counter and opened it up and poked his nose in it. A petite waitress in a dark brown uniform with yellow fringe on it approached Robin. She looked over the counter at him and asked, "Would you like some coffee?"

"Sure," he told her.

"I'll be right back with that. Do you need some more time to look over the menu?"

"Yes I do," he quickly replied.

Her face was round and snow white with two large patches of red blush on them. She wore a lipstick which had almost a purplish hue to it. The waitress gave Robin a slight smile, then said to him, "I'll be back with your coffee in a minute."

McElroy had already dipped his face back into the menu folder, ignorant of her more than usual notice of him. She must've been single, maybe nineteen or twenty years old. And looking.

When she came back with his coffee a minute later, The New Lone Ranger immediately informed her, "I'm ready to order."

"What will you have this morning?" the girl asked with a pleasant smile crossing her purple lips.

"Special Number Two."

"How would you like your eggs?"

"Over-easy."

"Bacon or sausage?"

"Sausage."

"Toast or a biscuit?"

"Biscuit."

"Thank you," she finally said. She flashed another teasing smile at the man wearing the black leather jacket. Somehow, she seemed to know that he was not some kind of "hard-ass." That black leather jacket was just a facade for a sweet and gentle man who seemingly had a way with women. John Travolta. Despite the fact he may have been gentle and caring, there was no overlooking the fact that he was, indeed, a real man. He was definitely not one of the boys.

Robin suddenly thought of something after she had walked away. He wanted some orange juice too, but she had failed to ask and he had failed to order. He had to be sure to order a large glass of orange juice the next time she came around. While he waited for his breakfast to be served, he pulled over a circular glass ash tray on the counter and lit up a cigarette.

A man in a spotless blue uniform, wearing a badge on his chest, a blue vi-sored cap on his head, a brown billy-club dangling from one side of his belt and a black holster shrouding a .357 magnum on the other side, entered the cafe. His presence demanded respect. The "Boy in Blue" reconnoitered the area, then took a seat at the swivel chair right next to Robin. McElroy's heart sank. His mind's eye immediately focused upon the suitcase of money back in his hotel room. How did he find out!? Not here! Not now! Robin nervously started tapping his foot on the orange tile floor. The officer turned to look at him, then gazed down at his tapping foot. The same waitress who came to Robin approached the police officer with her pad and pen already in hand.

"What'll it be today, Ollie?" the waitress asked the policeman in a tone of voice not quite up to par for being as pleasant as the one she'd spoken to Robin in.

"Special Number Three," he told her. "You know the way I like it. I'll have a black coffee and a small orange juice too."

"How's your wife?" the waitress added.

"She's still looking for a job," the policeman told her.

"Coming right up," she finally said.

McElroy forced himself to stop tapping his foot. His mind was racing. He noticed the officer didn't seem to be taking notice of him. Robin knew he didn't have his picture hanging in any post office; he'd never been convicted of anything. But what did this policeman know? Anything? Why did he sit right next to him when there were at least fifty other places to sit in this entire cafe? His heart was thumping hard inside of his sweatshirt. He wanted to walk out of the cafe right then and there, regardless of his breakfast order, but if he did that, he might look conspicuous. He knew he would look conspicuous. He suddenly wished he'd brought a newspaper so he could dip his face into it. Nervously, Robin McElroy puffed on his cigarette.

In another moment, his order was served. The reasonably attractive waitress with the purple lips placed an oval-shaped white dish before him had two eggs, their yolks now appearing "flesh-colored," three links of gray and "rust-colored" sausage, off-white and rust-brown hash browns and a very light tan-colored biscuit on it.

"Could I also have a large glass of orange juice?" McElroy put in.

"Sure."

This time the waitress didn't smile. She looked him over with a bit of skepticism. Was it a game? Her lower lip had dropped and there was a seemingly "caustic" twist to it. So what! Robin had decided already that he was not interested. When you look at the game from that angle, the only one who could possibly lose would be her.

Taking notice of the policeman who had just watched him receive his breakfast, the fork slipped out of his hand the first time he took hold of it.

"There's nothing to worry about," he told himself.

If that policeman had known who he was, for sure he would've said something by now. McElroy realized he was looking at a good five to ten years at least for a first offense. The cop continued to look him over, then shifted his glance towards the restaurant's kitchen quarters. Relief!

Temporary relief. Robin dug into his meal.

He sprinkled some salt and pepper on his eggs which had been done over-easy. He cut the links of sausage with his fork and wolfed them down. The policeman still hadn't said a word. Maybe he wouldn't? Maybe everything was "cool"? But what about the fact that this policeman had blatantly taken the seat right beside him when he entered this restaurant? Something was rotten in Denmark. While Robin sipped on his piping hot coffee, he thought to himself, "I want a divorce from this place."

Next, he took a gulp of his orange juice which had just been delivered without a word. He immersed himself in the sounds of silverware clattering into the dishwasher in the kitchen; waitresses taking and calling off orders; eggs sizzling on a skillet and the familiar ring of the cash register behind him. The policeman, nonetheless, was still seated beside him.

McElroy's mind's eye focused back upon the ebony-colored door to his hotel room. He could see in white letters, Number 23. There were two men, one clad in a tan-colored winter coat and the other one in a dismal gray one. They were both wearing hats to match their coats. The one in the tan knocked upon his door. He could see himself answering that knock from atop his bed with a "Who is it?"

"Police. Open up!"

Robin was at a loss for words. He suddenly protested, "You've got the wrong man."

"Alias Robin McElroy," the plainclothes policeman in the tan coat said to him. "We've got a warrant for your arrest."

His heart sank again. At the breakfast counter at Rubin Paccino's Italian Café, The New Lone Ranger's eyes were rolling in a frenzy while he ate his breakfast. Was the cop noticing anything abnormal about this man? He did not dare even look his way.

The waitress served the policeman his order and asked, "Will there be anything else?"

"No," he told her.

"Enjoy." the waitress added. Apparently, this "Ollie the Cop" was a most welcome customer at Rubin Paccino's Italian Café. He should be, Robin then thought. He maintains law and order in it. Some places in town probably even give him free meals.

McElroy drained his glass of orange juice, then started cutting up his over-easy eggs with his fork. The yellow yolks oozed open on the plate. He wolfed down the eggs as fast as he could without looking conspicuous. Every second he was aware of the fact this lawman was seated within a couple feet of him. All he would have to do is lean over and slap on the handcuffs if he wanted to. Maybe, Robin thought, he should even leave the hash browns and just get the hell out of this place? No. That would be a waste of good food. He told himself again, "The officer is not going to arrest me. If he was going to arrest me, he'd have done it by now."

The policeman was now starting on his meal and seemed oblivious to this fugitive. Robin cut up his hash browns with his fork, then stuffed them into his mouth. They were greasy. In a minute, they were gone and all he had left was his coffee and his biscuit. He finished off his cup of coffee, and as the wait-ress came by, about ready to ask him if he wanted a refill, McElroy stuttered, "Just the bill."

The waitress plucked out his bill from the apron in her uniform and handed it to him. Robin quickly looked it over. He plinked three quarters onto the counter and climbed to his feet. His legs were shaking. The policeman took a look at him from the midst of his meal. He's going to talk to me now, Robin imagined. Instead, after looking him over one more time, the policeman just looked back down at his plate and resumed eating his meal.

While he approached the cash register in the cafe, his heart was still pounding rapidly. Agony and uncertainty were scrawled across his visage.

"How was your meal?" the cashier asked him pleasantly. She was an over-weight black woman.

"G…Good," Robin replied. He felt as if his teeth were about to start chattering.

The woman at the cash register failed to take notice of the fact her patron was peeved about something. After looking up from her keyboard on the com-puterized machine, she told him, "Thanks. Come again." Her voice remained pleasant, as if everything had been said and done automatically with no regard for real sensitivity.

McElroy looked back one more time at the policeman to see if he was coming his way. The officer was still eating breakfast. Robin forced himself out through the revolving door to the cafeteria onto a city street. When the cold air from the street hit him, he felt a flush of relief go through his entire body. He strode quickly back towards the hotel. There were still lots of other people on this city street during this cold day in March. The skies were gray and overcast. The rain and snow had stopped falling. When he rounded the corner onto Halsted Street, he felt yet a greater sense of freedom. His stride was still at a quick cadence. He figured for sure by now he'd lost that cop.

Robin suddenly realized, while he was hiking south on Halsted Street, that everywhere he went he was going to have to live with this. This neighborhood had its share of policemen, just like any other neighborhood. He just thanked God that his picture wasn't hanging in every post office in the country. If it had been, no doubt he'd be riding down to the police station in a squad car right this minute. Up to this point, he had no police record. Still. Was there any way they could find out about him? He'd changed cities; that was a plus. He'd change cities in another month if he had to. If he sensed the heat was on, he'd "book" in a minute's notice.

The yellow and red-lettered sign, reading "The Saint James Hotel" came into view as he rounded the corner off of Halsted Street onto his own avenue. His final breath of relief was expelled when he spotted that sign. That sign was already home to him. He approached it quickly. When he entered through the black door at the entrance, he felt for sure now he was safe. He filed past the registration area and up the enclosed staircase to the second floor. While unlocking the door to his hotel room, a woman came out of the door next to him from the west. Her room number was Number 24. She looked the new tenant over carefully, but all Robin noticed about her was that she was a woman, probably in her late twenties. She was by no means a beauty queen, but not prohibitively ugly either. She was medium in build. She was still studying The New Lone Ranger until he disappeared into his room. Neither one of them said hello.

The woman immediately wondered why her new neighbor didn't even bother to say "hello" to her. Was he married? Single? Why didn't he have a "hard-on" for her as so many other men did? She was intrigued by his evasive glance. It was not shyness, she detected. It was reticence. But why?

When he got inside of his hotel room, he turned the key in the lock and put on the deadbolt. The woman could hear the deadbolt being latched through the door. "So he wants his privacy," she said to herself. Robin half expected that woman to come knocking on his door after him. Instead, he heard her footsteps walk by on the concrete in the hallway past it, and then he heard them start clumping down the stairs. His ear was now resting against the black door.

McElroy quickly slid open his bottom drawer to see if the small suitcase was still there. It was. He was free at last! Or was he? He lay down upon his bed and lit up another cigarette. If the police didn't get him, there was the party he'd stolen the money from. They would just love to get their hands on this "Christian Crook." If they ever did get their hands on him, they'd for certain "cancel his ticket" or give him "the deep six treatment."

Chapter Five

He didn't see her again until a month later. Their brief, non-vocal, yet somewhat "tacit" interlude in the hallway had not been forgotten by Robin. He hadn't much to think about anyway during all the days he spent cooped up in his hotel room listening to the radio or oftentimes just doing nothing. Not much was happening in Robin McElroy's life these days, and he was perfectly happy just to keep it that way.

By the time the spring season was in full swing during the month of April, Robin spent almost every afternoon out in Manteno Park. He sat on a green, wooden park bench and watched the children at play on the basketball court. An old man who'd lost his eyesight and walked with a red and white-striped cane passed him by at the same time every day he was seated on that bench. A few people at this time of year, on warmer days, lay out a blanket and had a picnic in the park. A patrolman usually ambulated past him on the sidewalk at the same time every day. Nobody ever bothered to say hi. To McElroy, that was probably for the better.

While seated on the park bench, he smoked cigarette after cigarette. Robin McElroy may have been deemed a chain smoker. He just could not do without those "little devils." Occasionally he'd look over towards that yellow and red-lettered sign which read "The Saint James Hotel." Its presence simply could not be parried. He would look over at it sometimes, then he would have to direct his glance that way again. It was unavoidable. He wore his cross necklace every day, without fail. It was a part of him. Nobody could take that away from him. Nobody. He wore the same black-cleated cowboy boots every day, and the same black leather jacket. The cross, the boots, and the jacket were all a part of his character. His odd character. He was an anomaly.

He had four pairs of blue jeans which he wore on rotation. His apparel included three different sweaters, a checked flannel shirt, and four cotton short-sleeved summer shirts. He had an abundance of underpants and T-shirts. Socks? There were eight different pairs in assorted colors, three of them blue.

He gazed upon that sign one more time which read "The Saint James Hotel." To him, there was something "catchy" about that sign. Was it the colors? Was it the name? Was it because that was where he lived? He didn't even know himself.

There was a swing set in Manteno Park. Sometimes Robin would sit in the rubber seat of the swing and hold onto the metal chains suspending it. He'd kick his feet in the dirt, then push and pump while he swung back-and-forth on it. The ride would eventually make him slightly dizzy. It was all that body pollution from his cigarettes nauseating him which caused that. Carbon monoxide. Nicotine. Those poisons were rampant in his bloodstream. At that time, he'd kick his heels in the dirt and come to a halt. It was child's fun, anyway, he thought.

Trees. Big green trees grew in that park. At this time of the year, they were just beginning to develop their leaves. The grass had turned green and would soon need to be mowed. There were also a couple of monuments in that park. Statues of long-forgotten war heroes who once served this country. The steel had an ugly blue coating on them, tarnished by the foul air. Nonetheless, the monuments stood proud in that park.

Robin always kept a switchblade tucked away in the pocket of his blue jeans. Most likely if a situation ever occurred where he'd require it, he'd most likely be afraid to use it. Who, then, was this unmasked man wearing the big bold cross? He didn't want to kill anybody. And who's to say it was going to save his life if his attacker was carrying a gun?

He had found a Laundromat to do his wash at every Friday. His clothes never stunk. Maybe that was one lesson which had carried over from his mother? At the Laundromat, nobody socialized with him. The city was just the right place for Robin McElroy. He figured if people were to start asking him questions such as: "Where do you work?" "Where do you come from?" Etc.; he'd get caught up in a mess of lies that would become impossible to untangle. And if once he was found to be a liar, it might arouse suspicion. Robin knew the best thing to do as a fugitive was to keep to himself. As a last resort, lying would have to be the thing to do. It was an Unchristian thing to do. But didn't this man have to look out for Number One before deliberately throwing himself to the wolves?

Rubin Paccino's Café was the spot to eat. Its prices were reasonable, and after that first day he went there, the cop he'd encountered never sat next to him again. He did see him in there a couple of times since, but he was no longer deathly afraid of him. He didn't have his "number."

Apparently, this fugitive had found a temporary haven of safety on the south side of Chicago. He knew in his own mind he wouldn't be there forever. He must someday move on. Just because it was safe now didn't mean that Chicago would always be a safe place for him to hide. The Feds were looking for him. They didn't know his real name. That was a plus. Robin McElroy had even entered the town he committed the heist in under a fictitious name. He was a mastermind. He thought he was a mastermind. Really. Just how much did the Feds know about the elusive Robin McElroy?

The sun was shining bright on this April afternoon. Pigeons ambled along the sidewalk and in the grass looking for a handout or morsels of food that had been left behind. They would strut within a couple feet of him. The sky up above was blue, but a dirty hue of blue. There was pollution in the air. Clouds heavily littered the skies. It blocked out a good portion of the yellow rays being emitted by the sun. The bright white ball in the sky had a hazy sheen between it and this particular portion of the earth.

Robin also noticed that a street gang had been out "painting the park" the night before. Spray-painted in blue letters on a park bench, it read "Eat Shit." On the sidewalk, in red letters it read "The Sheiks Rule The South Side." Farther down the sidewalk, in black-colored spray paint, it read in big, bold letters "The Pink Hole is #1." In blue letters, again, on the sidewalk even farther south yet, it read "Dope Can Get You Through Times Of No Money—But Money Can't Get You Through Times Of No Dope." The sidewalk in Manteno Park, in other words, was an elaborate mess. He also surmised that one would not find "the answer" in Manteno Park either.

McElroy torched another cigarette and looked back at the sign that read "The Saint James Hotel." It was a colorful, yet dull and lifeless thing. The light inside remained on all the time. And the white of the light could be seen shining through the holes. It beckoned him to look at it, while it loomed above that black door.

He cast his glance the other way and noted the building south of Manteno Park, directly opposite his living quarters, which was being constructed. From where he sat on that green bench in the park, he could hear the clatter of machinery and tools banging away to put the building together. Men in light brown work clothes toiled away endlessly. They wore scarlet-colored hardhats. Sometimes they could be heard yelling at each other. Robin decided that men in construction lead a hard life. The month before, he noted they had a fire burning in front of the building designed to keep them warm when they drew near it. That fire wasn't needed in April. A huge pile of debris littered the front of the site. It was a hard life, indeed, he reckoned.

McElroy finally figured he'd better be getting back to his room. The sun was beginning to dip behind the trees in the park. It would be dark in another hour. He strolled back towards the hotel along the sidewalk in the park. He crossed over some of the street gang graffiti and set his sights north. He looked back at his bench. Would it remain vacant until tomorrow when he returned to it? Or would some bum, maybe an alcoholic from skid row, make a bed of it that evening? Who knows? Who cares?

He looked both ways before crossing the street he lived on to The Saint James Hotel. The traffic on this street was usually light. He crossed it. Upon entering under the yellow sign through the black door, he noticed his woman neighbor from room Number 24 was entering in the hotel behind him. She followed him through the alcove and up the staircase to the second floor. When he got to the top of the staircase, the sound of her footsteps stopped and her voice cracked the air.

"What does a girl have to do to get together with you?" she asked him.

Robin spun his head, surprised at first. Did he ever suspect she was going to break the ice? He looked her over carefully. Even in the dark of the staircase, he could see her brown hair with a reddish tinge to it. She had a ghost-white face, with a smattering of freckles. The girl had a pug nose and brown eyes that were her most outstanding features. Her brownish-red hair tumbled over her shoulders. McElroy could see it all because of the light in the second-floor hallway at the top of the stairs.

A slight smile finally crossed his face. She was just a girl. She was most likely filled with immature ideas that were outlandish to him. He thought she was a woman the first time he saw her coming out of her door. Sometimes first impressions deceive. She was a girl. So what!?

"Just knock on my door," he told her.

Chapter Six

After offering that invitation to his strange neighbor, Robin wondered what might become of it. Anything? Had he made a mistake? Would he be able to get her out of his life if he needed to? It remained engraved in his head bone that she lived just next door to him. The New Lone Ranger had known for the past twelve years that he was a "magnet" to women. He was quite aware of the matrimonial stakes and the fact that women in general could often be quite dangerous. He locked the door behind him and put on the deadbolt, then walked across his hotel room and switched on the Panasonic radio. He wanted to forget about what he had just done. If she was going to take him up on what he had said, she was going to do it. Reticence. That was the key. He was going to keep his distance from this "newfound friend." He wasn't going to let her get under his skin. He was not going to reveal his entire life's story to her. He must remain aloof and tactful.

The afternoon disc-jockey, Rick Zachary, was on Chicago's Big 96 at this time. Robin turned up the volume on his coal-colored unit. It was as if the DJ was living inside of the damned thing. He was talking through a hole in it. That machine was as black as the throughs of hell. And all the disc-jockeys were living in it. McElroy thought he had been redeemed via his lifestyle. He was free of society's toxicity. He was out of that "rat race jungle" in which only the rats could win. He was as free as a seagull flying aimlessly over the ocean. Was this young lady next door going to interfere with his karma"?

Robin lay back atop his bed and lit up another cigarette. The tip of the "white cancer stick" glowed orange. Grayish white smoke drifted off the end of it rising into the still air of his hotel room. His hotel room reeked of the stench of cigarette smoke, yet Robin McElroy was barely aware of it due to the fact his sense of smell had been greatly dulled by the dangerous habit.

Maybe the stench of his butts would help to repel this neighbor who most likely was going to try to weave her way into his life. At the same time, Robin McElroy would always be trying to "ween" her away. His mind's eye drifted him back into another time in his life. He saw himself as a young man in his early twenties. He was laboring in a factory. It was three dollars an hour work in his hometown in Kansas. "Pauper's Pay." He cast his glance across the room to the drawer of which the suitcase loaded with Ulysses S. Grant's portraits was secured. The combination lock suitcase in there entered his mind's eye. Once again, his thought pattern shifted to that factory he was working in as a young man of about twenty-two years. The year was 1972. He knew by this time he was a "ladies' man." He had finally begun to find himself. Robin was weening his way away from the boys.

They no longer had anything worthwhile to say to him. But he worked in that factory with them. It was all men in that factory. They made fun of him; sometimes they became agitated with him. It was no fun working there. The soot. The heat. The profanity. He was living in hell.

Finally. Finally he had been "released." His cherry-colored Chevy, a 1961 Impala in respectable condition, waited out in the factory's parking lot for him every day. When he finished his work there at 4:30, he walked out to it alone. Always alone. He reckoned he'd paid his dues to society.

While he was dreaming, his mind suddenly focused to the present. There he was, alone in his hotel room at the sleazy Saint James Hotel in Chicago. But he was free.

He looked over at the black radio unit on the floor of his room. And listened.

"Rick Zachary here with you on Chicago's Big 96, WZMX until six o'-clock. Two years ago today this song made it onto Chicago's Hot 100. Does time fly or what? I can remember playing this song every day while it became a gold hit for the Pointer Sisters. Here's 'Slow Hand,' on WZMX...."

Robin's train of thought, while the song played, traveled back in time again to the year 1972. He was parked in his vermillion-colored 1961 Chevy with a long, white decorative band on it between the chrome. It was a two-door hard-top. Flashy. New paint. Old engine. This Impala was parked out alone on a seldom-ventured country road in Kansas. It was nighttime. There was a short, chubby girl of nineteen years with short brown hair seated in the back seat with Robin. She was nude above the waist of her "hip-hugger" blue jeans. Her belt buckle remained fastened. There were tears streaming down her cheeks while she was talking to Robin, who was wearing a pasty and sheepish look on his face while she talked. His mouth was open with awe. He was not able to cope with the situation confronting him.

"I've always wanted to get married and raise a family, ya know, like my mom did," she was saying. "We've bin going out a while. You're a real sweet guy, ya know. You got a nice little job. I kin work for my dad." She sniffed. "You're a real nice guy…." Her lips were trembling. She had finally mustered up enough courage to let the cat out of the bag. And Robin was stunned!

In the light of the Kansas Moon, her two breasts were illuminated in the back seat of the car. They were an "ivory-colored mirage" in his mind. Her right breast was slightly larger than the left one. A pair of large, dark brown nipples protruded from them. He cast his young eyes down upon those bosoms, then returned to look into her tearful eyes. He whispered when he spoke, vividly recalling the relationship with Mary LaTella which had ended not too long before he met this girl.

"But we're not in love," he told her. "We're not in love. That makes a big difference."

The brown-haired girl sniffed again, then rubbed one of her eyes with her right hand.

"It done matter," she replied. "We'll get along. I know we will. You just gotta realize that I need a man like my mother did to marry and raise a family."

Robin's thought shifted temporarily from this melodrama playing in his mind to the song on the radio in his room at The Saint James Hotel. The song "Slow Hand," by the Pointer Sisters, was still playing over WZMX. He listened to a few passages from it, then returned to "dreamland."

He was staring at her bare breasts again in the moonlight. The nipples were hard. Protruding. She was very nervous, yet sexually excited as well. She wanted to give him her all, yet not until they got married.

"We kin make it," she pleaded. "I know I shouldn't be askin', but you're such a sweet guy. We kin work it out. I know we can."

Robin had never been under so much pressure in his young life. Should he give this girl his John Hancock? It would be like signing his life away. What about the real love he'd once known? Mary LaTella. This girl could never replace Mary LaTella. She couldn't even carry her "jock-strap"!

"No!" exclaimed Robin in the back seat of his red Chevy. "No! No! No!" He shook his head vehemently. "Now I'm taking you home right now! This is not going to work out! I'm not in love!"

At the relatively young age of twenty-two years, Robin McElroy had already quite adeptly learned to walk like a man. This trait would never leave him. If something didn't seem right to him, he was not going to be a patsy and not speak his mind. Even then, Robin McElroy was by no means a "yes man."

His attention resumed his focus upon the radio playing in his hotel room. "Slow Hand," by the Pointer Sisters, was finishing its play on it. He looked over at the chest of drawers across the room from him. All the money he needed for the remainder of his life was encased in that unit. Once again, he resumed his travel through The Land of Enchantment.

He could see his mother standing in the kitchen of their Kansas home in her white flowered dress again. Her wizened suntanned face was talking to him.

"Do in Rome as the Romans do," his mother was telling young Robin. Bullshit! That's what Robin thought. He would do as he damned well pleased! His mother was wrong again. Degradation! Crap! He wasn't going to listen to her anymore. Her "do in Rome" philosophy held no water with Robin McElroy. He was going to do what he wanted to do. It's impossible to please everybody anyways.

The only person he really cared to please was himself. Maybe, then, it was time for Robin McElroy to move on?

Unless a movie was "Walt Disney," it was too "hard-core" for his "Mennonite Mother" to deal with. Robin was about to make the scene on another type of program, and he didn't need his mother, the girl who wanted to marry him, or the boys at the factory to get in his way!

Chapter Seven

The day following his second encounter with his next-door neighbor in Room 24, he heard three light knocks on his bedroom door. Who else could it be but her? He answered the door from his leisurely spot atop his bed and saw her standing there in the hallway. She flashed a quick, uneasy smile at him, then asked, "Can I come in?"

McElroy stepped aside for her and she entered. He knew women. Generally, they all think the same, just like most men do. With men, it's usually sex. With women, the issues are usually either the money or security in a marriage. The gauntlet had already been tossed; was Robin McElroy ready to meet the challenge?

Evening was falling over the City of Chicago. It was a Friday. It had been raining earlier that day. Robin figured she had probably just gotten off from work.

"Where do you work?" he quickly asked while taking a moderate interest while delivering the question. She ignored his question temporarily while she scanned the premise for a place to sit. There was none. "You don't have a chair in here?"

"They didn't include one with the room," McElroy answered.

"They did with mine," the girl put in.

"You can sit on my bed," Robin offered.

"My name is Cynthia Craig."

She took delicate strides around the room, not so sure yet she wanted to take a seat upon his bed next to him.

"Robin McElroy."

Cynthia nodded in approval, taking a place to stand on the west side of his chest of drawers. There was a portable refrigerator, now, on the floor beside her feet. Robin had a rental on it, finding it very useful in regards to the fact that he didn't like to eat out three meals a day.

"You like it here?" Miss or Missus Craig inquired. Robin didn't know at this point in time whether or not this new acquaintance was a miss or a missus. Her eyes met his when she asked the question, then drifted away out his hotel room window. She was beginning to seem nervous to him while she stood there leaning against the chest of drawers. He remained standing by the door. It was still open, in fact. She crossed her legs where she stood, putting the weight of her body on the right foot. She was still wearing her blue windbreaker which she most likely wore to work. There was an old white wool sweater under it. On her legs were a pair of blue jeans. Her jeans didn't fit that well. They appeared to be the type of jeans one would buy at discount store on sale. All of Robin's jeans were designer jeans. "It'll do for now," he replied.

"I work in the front office of The Beacon Furniture Manufacturing Company," she told him with a final regard towards answering his question. "It's an old company located on The South Side."

The conversation seemed to die right there. She moved across the room and placed her well-rounded bottom on the middle of his bed. She had taken notice of the fact that her neighbor had remained standing beside the open door to his hotel room. She must've figured by now that her neighbor was not the overpowering aggressive type. Good. She looked up to him again from his bed as if she was going to be receptive to any more of his conversation if he would just let it come. Robin was staring vacantly into his open closet on the west side of the room now, trying to evade her glance. He shifted his eyes back towards her for a quick moment, then asked, "Do you like it?"

"No," she replied bluntly.

There was a defined wire of sternness in her voice when she told him "no" to that question. The word was emphasized.

"Are you married?" Robin suddenly asked.

"Nope. Are you?"

"Not in my thirty-three years," he told her with a hint of challenge in his voice. He was watching her when he said that. He was probing for a facial reaction. However, she reacted to it, her facial expression hadn't changed and the way she felt about what he had said was shrouded to his knowledge.

Again, there was silence. This time it was an uneasy silence. Robin suddenly thought that just because they were neighbors, they didn't have to know each other. This girl was mysterious to him. Spooky. He already felt uncomfortable with her.

"So, you're single…." Robin repeated slowly, starting to feel again at a loss for words. He was probing her again with eyes, seeking the truth with more than a casual degree of interest.

"If I wasn't, I wouldn't be here." she finally said. That, she figured, was the best she could do for this inquisitive gentleman. It had become apparent to her now, upon looking into his eyes, that he was, indeed, searching for some kind of story between the lines. She also thought, after becoming aware of that, that maybe this fellow in the room next to her was more than just "one-dimensional." Good.

"I see," he added.

That pair of brown eyes now were staring a hole through him while he stood at the open doorway. He measured that "ghost-white" face again, and that patch of freckles across her nose and cheeks. He figured she was too old for freckles. His train of thought, now, was beginning to wander from the conversation they were having.

"Do you work?" she asked him, a bit curious this time. Her curiosity was this time detected by McElroy.

That was an important factor, wasn't it, he thought. If he told her "no," he may never see her again.

"No."

He wanted to leave it at that. If she was going to pursue it any further, he would have to start defending himself with myriads of lies. He was already prepared to do that if he had to.

"Where do you get your money?"

The trick to telling a lie, Robin always knew, was to "believe it" before you tell it. His thought process, he suddenly knew, had to be accelerated.

"I have enough of it stored away so I don't have to work," Robin explained. He wasn't exactly telling her a lie, just not the whole truth.

"Then what are you doing here?" She was examining him further. That last answer had just generated a new plateau of interest. He felt a little bit uneasy this time she inquired. He grasped for an explanation.

"Personal reasons," he suddenly answered.

"I wish I were you," she blurted out. "Never having to work. You've got the system beat!"

"Really," McElroy said, noting her burst of enthusiasm. He could see she was on his side. "It's a boring life."

"It sure beats slaving for some hardnosed boss who doesn't appreciate the work you do for him and is always trying to get you in bed."

"I'm sorry," Robin replied, quickly.

Actually, he couldn't have cared less. She was still nobody to him. She may have been on his side now, because he was a single man with some money. Yes. That the point she was making to The New Lone Ranger now.

She was thinking maybe she'd found a gem amongst this pile of junk she lived in. He didn't have to work!

He was still young. And he was handsome! There was no denying that. This relationship must go on, she decided.

He was even a gentleman! What had she done to deserve this? She was thinking now, how am I going to "weave" my way into his life?

"Do you get high?" she asked.

"No."

"You really should," she carried on. "It makes everything look a lot better. You wouldn't get so bored around here all day every day if you got high."

"I don't need it," he told her.

"It wouldn't seem so boring around here if you did get high," she added again. "I'm serious. You could go crazy in here if you stayed straight all the time."

Now she had hit a raw nerve with him. That wasn't right. She was making a mistake. This time he raised his voice when he talked to her.

"The answer is no. I'm really not interested."

"I just like to toot a little coke on weekends …."

She was pleading this time. She wanted to establish this foundation between them and make it imperative he see her more often.

"I don't want to hear any more about it. Drop the subject!" McElroy's voice was firm.

Cynthia let out a deep breath from atop his bed.

He still hadn't moved away from that door, she noticed.

Did he want to? She looked into his eyes for some kind of explanation to that question. He sure talked like a man, she thought. There was a long moment of silence again between them. He even looked like a man. Yes! This guy was really something! He was a must for her to have!

"Are you planning on sticking around?" she asked.

"For a while," he replied.

There was a smile which crossed her pink-colored lips now. She'd carefully applied some lipstick to them before leaving for work that day. She had been anticipating this visit with her new neighbor all day. Revealed in that smile was a front tooth which was slightly chipped. She didn't have the money to pay a dentist to re-cap it.

"I'm glad we're neighbors," she finally said.

"I'm glad too," Robin replied, still not really caring. It was just an off-the-cuff statement. Her enthusiasm for him, to him, was quite lucid at this point in time. The feeling, at least not sincerely, was not being returned. He had remained aloof.

"Would you like a glass of milk or fruit juice?" he quickly asked.

"Fruit juice," she told him.

McElroy slid open the top drawer of his dresser and produced a clear plastic vessel. He went to the refrigerator and filled it with fruit juice, then handed it to Miss Craig.

"I'm going to buy a percolator tomorrow so I can have some coffee," he added. "I've already found this refrigerator most useful."

"I drink about eight cups of coffee a day at work," she put in. "It's free."

"Then I'm certain you won't want any of mine," Robin tried to joke.

"No. That's okay," she said, "I'll have some of yours too. Coffee keeps me going."

She had failed to comprehend his attempt at humor. Was there any humor in her life? That was yet to be known by Robin.

Again, McElroy noticed the implication towards the use of a drug. Only it was coffee this time. Eight cups a day! He was beginning to get the picture with her in that respect. Maybe she was just looking for a "friend," he thought for a moment. What kind of friend? Was she going to try to get in with him for a share of his money? He thought about that. Maybe she was just some kind of a "gold-digger"? She was not unpleasant to be with, on the other side of the coin. Maybe he should spend a little time and money on her? To him, again, she seemed sort of "girlish." At this point, he noted the fact his train of thought was once again starting to wander while she sat there somewhat nervously on his bed. Robin remained standing at the open door to his room.

"How long have you lived in this hotel?" he finally asked after a long pause.

"Almost two years."

"Can't you do any better than this? You're working, you know."

She became defensive at what he had just said. It sounded a bit rude to her. What was his game? The real reason she had no money was because she spent a large amount of her paycheck on cocaine. There was nothing left to pay the rent at a more expensive living quarters.

"I don't want to," she lied.

"You don't want to?" he asked, prying a little deeper. "Why not?"

Cynthia noticed the man in him coming out again. He certainly wasn't her fool. She paused. At least he wasn't her fool yet! He interested her. Here was a man who didn't want anything from anybody, she figured. There were no "sexual waves or vibrations" flowing between them yet at this late date. Oh no! Was he gay? Well. If he was gay, maybe that wouldn't be so bad either. They could still be friends. She groped for an answer to his question.

"Really," she explained. "I don't have enough money to live anyplace better. This place will do. I'm surviving."

The need for money had surfaced. First she was trying to get him interested in her drugs. Now she was explaining that even with her front office job she was unable to do any better than The Saint James Hotel. What was wrong with that picture? Was she a scam or not?

Miss Craig drained her glass of fruit juice and placed the plastic cup on the floor of the room at her feet. He decided he was not going to ask her if she wanted some more. He'd seen enough of her for today. Her interest in him, after those prying questions, had waned a bit. He would be "tougher" to deal with than she thought. "Tougher to milk." That was more like it. He was neat. Was he any kind of a prospect to marry? She couldn't tell from this first interlude, but he'd already laid some pretty nice cards upon the table. The silence between them was extremely lengthy this time. At that point, she sensed maybe it was time to go home.

"One more thing before I go," she put in quickly. Her nervousness, which was apparent initially, had dissolved completely. "I was wondering if you could put my laundry in with yours if you're doing it tomorrow or Sunday. I'm going away this weekend. I could just bring it over to your room right now…."

Robin cut her off.

"I'm not doing my laundry this weekend," he told her. "Also," he added, "I'm used to giving orders, not taking them. If that's quite all right with you?" There was a grating in his voice this time. Strength. And a touch of anger. His eyes lit up when he spoke those words. It was at that time that Cynthia realized he could really take or leave her without any remorse. She ducked her head under his escalated tone of voice.

"I'm sorry," she stuttered. Her lower lip was trembling now. "I'll be going now." She stood up from the bed and ambulated across the hotel room. After passing through the still open door, she looked back in on him flashing her chipped tooth smile.

"Good-bye. It was nice to meet you," she said.

"Good-bye." Robin added, then pushed the door behind her slowly and closed it. He removed the key from his pocket, twisted it in the lock, then put on the deadbolt. It was an eventful encounter for him. And she was every bit as "girlish" as he had anticipated she would be.

Chapter Eight

At Rubin Paccino's Italian Café that evening, Robin McElroy was served by a corpulent waitress in brown with yellow fringe. He was eating a bowl of chili. It was the cheapest dinner the cafe offered, being listed at $1.65 a bowl. He had a tall glass of milk to drink. He needed his milk. There was a side order of pasta salad costing him 1.50. The milk was seventy-five cents. Cheap eating. He smoked a cigarette while he ate at the counter where he usually sat. While he was perched upon that chrome stool with an orange-colored padded seat, a short young man of about 5'2" moved in next to him. He was wearing his hair in close to a crew-cut; his face was cut in half by a pair of rectangular-shaped wire-rim glasses. His hair was black in color, and provocatively close-cropped. His build was slender. When you put that conglomeration of observations into perspective, the guy sitting next to him was the epitome of a "twerp." He looked over The New Lone Ranger with beady, insecure eyes behind the rather thick lenses of his optical gear.

"Hi," he said to Robin, softly.

McElroy turned to look at him from his dinner.

Hadn't he seen this "leaping gnome" in this place before? Yes. And he'd been studying Robin the other time he'd seen him there too.

"Hi," he finally replied.

"Nice place, huh?" the person in crew cut asked.

"The food is good," Robin told him.

There was a long pause before anything else was said. McElroy returned to eating his meal. His aloofness was not overlooked by the newcomer. He was playing some kind of game with him, wasn't he? That's what the guy in the wire-rims thought.

"Ricky McKlaskey." the runt offered, extending his right hand to shake. When The New Lone Ranger noticed this guy's hand was extended, in return he offered his hand only to shake. Not to pet!

After another long moment of silence, the boy in the crew cut asked him. "What's your name?"

McElroy hesitated. He did not really want to carry on a conversation with the young fellow. There was really, through his own eyes, nothing this boy could tell him that would really ever be of any value to him.

"Robin McElroy." he finally said.

McKlaskey smiled. It was a sunny sort of smile. Was he going to break the ice with him or not? There was some kind of facade about this McElroy, wasn't there, he thought.

While he resumed threading his fork through his chili, the "twerp" studied him some more. There was an overabundance over interest behind those wire-rims. Robin had already taken note of that. He raised his glass of milk and took a sip. At that time, the same waitress who'd waited on McElroy came to McKlaskey.

"Would you like something to drink?" she asked him.

"What kind of soft drinks do you have?" the boy asked.

"Coke. Pepsi. 7-Up. And Sprite."

"I'll take some milk just like he has," Ricky suddenly told her oddly. The fat waitress crinkled her right eyebrow. She was thinking the same thing that Robin was thinking at that time. He's a very strange boy.

"Milk, then," she said, "I'll be right back with it." She turned her back to him, then looked over her shoulder and asked Ricky curtly, "Are you sure you can pay for it?"

"Yes," McKlaskey told her. He rifled through his pockets and produced his wallet, then spread it apart at the top and flashed several "greenbacks" from inside of it. He added an uncertain smile when he looked up at her. Apparently, his reputation around Rubin Paccino's Italian Café was not the best. The waitress nodded, then strutted away. When she was gone, the focus of his attention was her eye. Robin took note of the flaming red sport shirt he was wearing. It was short-sleeved. His black windbreaker was draped over the orange-padded seat of the stool he was seated upon. He certainly is "flaming," McElroy surmised.

"Like it in Chicago?" Ricky asked casually.

"No," Robin told him. His answer was straight-forward and blunt. McKlaskey immediately pursed his lips taking note of the blatant lack of interest this man was returning in him. Bah humbug and phooey on everybody, he must've been thinking.

"Have you got the time?" the boy asked, desperately trying to egg him on into a conversation. That was enough to get past Robin McElroy, who preferred eating his dinners in solitude rather than being accompanied by some kind of a "leech." It was perfectly apparent to Mr. McElroy what this young man was in search of. It was scrawled all across his face. He was in definite need of a "beef jerky" from this handsome "studly" brute.

"Listen, young fella," Robin told him with a jagged edge in his voice, "What you came here for and what I came here for are two totally different things. Now, I think we both know what I'm talking about. How would you like me to get on the phone right now and call the boys to come pick you up? You can explain the whole thing down at city hall, and I'm certain the boys in blue will be far more receptive to listening to what you have to say than I would be. Are we on the same level of communication now, young man?"

Robin McElroy was staring into his face the entire time he was saying this, and while talking to him, he could see the look on his face change from a look of zeal and attentiveness to mask of molten mass confusion in terror! Ricky's mouth was agape. Robin could see his tonsils, as a matter of fact. He was stunned just like a fish that had been struck over the head with an oar!

"You're…you're not a vice cop…are you?" Ricky stuttered. "If you are, I'm going to kill myself!"

"You'd probably be doing yourself a favor if you did!" McElroy snapped back at him.

That did it! Ricky slid off of his seat, scooped up his black windbreaker and reeled across the floor out the revolving door. He was gone in an instant. Just at that time, the corpulent waitress came to the counter with Ricky's milk.

"What happened to him?" she asked, taking note that he had rapidly disappeared out the revolving door. Robin thought for a moment before answering her, then said, "He just found out he needed a change of underwear."

Chapter Nine

Food for thought about employing the use of a chair in his hotel room was in Robin's "hopper." The actual carrying out of the purchase and installment of one had not yet materialized. In the meantime, McElroy continued to lie or sit atop his rickety bed. It was a Monday afternoon; it was the Monday after the Friday of which he had had his first visitation from Cynthia. She crossed his roaming mind periodically. He didn't ever think there could be any value for her as great as the value he'd once placed upon Mary LaTella.

The radio unit in his bedroom was playing. The volume on it was lower than usual, so not to disturb his train of thought. Rick Zachary was once again at the helm of Chicago's Big 96, WZMX. Robin liked Rick Zachary the best because his show included more oldies than any of the other disc-jockey's shows on WZMX. There was also a certain pep to the things Rick promoted. He was ringer so far as DJs went.

"In the Navy," by the Village People, was playing over the air at the time. Robin knew the Village People was an all-male group from New York which played "campy" disco music. They had always stood out in his mind for some particular reason. Rick played their music more often than ought to be warranted.

McElroy's thought pattern regressed to that Christmas Mary LaTella presented his cherished gold cross necklace. He could see the two of them standing beside the Christmas tree in her home in Kansas. She was wearing a fluffy white sweater and tailored maroon-colored slacks. She was as neat as a pin. Her apparel came from stores the likes of Lord and Taylor and Marshall Fields. So did that cross she presented him with during the Christmas of 1970. She was smiling a big white-toothed smile at young Robin while she presented him with the gift wrapped in cardinal-colored wrapping paper. McElroy could see himself removing the ribbon beside the tree and tearing off that wrapping paper. She was still smiling at him, with a twinkle in her mature womanly eyes. The wrapping paper was set upon the floor under the tree, and what was left was a rectangular ivory-colored box. He opened the top of the box, and there it was, in white stuffing. It was a beautiful gold cross necklace. It had to have been the most beautiful gift young Robin had ever received. It was just that previous summer, within the duration of his friendship with Mary, that young McElroy had discovered Christ. This helped confirm his belief, right then and there beside that Christmas tree in 1970, that Christ was as real as the sun that rises every morning. He could see Mary still smiling at him, taking the cross out of the box for him and draping it around his neck.

The New Lone Ranger exited dreamland with the conclusion of the song "In the Navy" and the sound of Rick. Zachary's voice over the coal-colored unit on the floor beside his bed.

"Four years ago today, that song was flying high on the charts for the Village People," Rick explained. "We've got a wonderful spring day out there."

"You'll be needing a light jacket or a sweater if you go outdoors. Tonight the mercury is going to be taking a nosedive as a result of a cold front moving in from Canada. Right now I've got 62 at O'Hare, 59 at the Lakefront and sixty-one degrees at WZMX. The time is 4:41 at WZMX.

"A friend of mine who I just talked to last night asked me if I'd play this certain hit for him. He said he hasn't heard it on this station in a while. There's a wee bit of dust on it, but it's by no means a 'moldy oldie'. Let's trip back in time to the year 1977 with platinum two-million seller for the group Queen, here's 'We Are the Champions', at WZMX…."

After that song came on, there was a knock at Robin's door. If the radio had been playing any louder, he most likely wouldn't have heard it. He rolled off of his bed and walked across his room. There was no doubt in his mind before he even answered it that it was Cynthia calling upon him again. He reckoned she'd probably be clinging to him as a barnacle does to a ship from now on. Maybe, he thought, before answering it, it was time to nip this thing in the bud? Maybe he should remove his ship from the sea and pilot it through "fresh water" for a while. When a boat does that, the barnacles always "slip off."

When he opened the black door, he could see Cynthia Craig standing in the gloomy second floor hallway of The Saint James Hotel. She smiled at him, slightly. That chipped front tooth was once again visible. She was wearing her neatly applied pink lipstick. Her eyes contained a noticeable hue of red in the whites. The same windbreaker was on her back, with a vermillion-colored cotton blouse underneath it. A different pair of "non-fitting" blue jeans clad her legs.

"Can I come in?" she asked.

"Okay," he replied, opening the black door wide enough so she could pass through it.

"Still no chair," she noticed upon reconnoitering the bedroom. It was if she had made a proposal for that the previous Friday, and her call should've been answered by Monday.

"Still no chair," Robin repeated.

She did a 180 degree turn to face him while standing on the west side of chest of drawers again. She looked atop the dresser and noticed the chrome percolator set upon it.

"I see you bought a percolator," she said.

"I did on Saturday. The coffee in it is cold. I turned it off...." he was saying.

"You can just plug it in again and heat it up. Don't waste it. I'm not choosey about the coffee I drink. The coffee at work could clean a radiator."

Robin smiled slightly at her jest.

"All right," he told her. He reached for the new brown-colored cord and plugged it into the wall unit to the west of the chest of drawers. He unintentionally brushed her blue jeans while inserting the plug into the socket near the floor.

"How was work?" he asked.

"Do you know any other boss who carries a jar of Vaseline to work with him?"

Her words iced through his mind. What she said had to have been planned and was intended to draw some kind of a reaction from Robin. She was watching his face while she said that. She was looking for either a grimace or pleasant curl to his lips or a flare in his eyeballs. The expression on his face remained placid. Like stone. There was positively no reaction to her implication that she did have an ass.

"Hope," he replied. "Have you ever decided to report sexual harassment to someone higher up?"

"And lose my job!" Cynthia exclaimed. "No way!"

"It's he who is creating the problem, not you," Robin told her.

In thinking, mulling over what McElroy had just said, she figured he had some kind of sensitivity to him which was uncommon in most males. Her first impression of his being "a must to have" was being re-confirmed.

"I don't know what to do about it. I feel so unwanted and uncomfortable there," she explained.

Now Robin detected that she was looking for sympathy from him; not necessarily consolation. And he probably had the money to get her out of this predicament if he got to know her better. Yes, the money matter was going to surface every time she came here.

"It's your problem, not mine," he said. "Do what you want with it."

His words were firm. He had given her the brush in as subtle a way as he possibly could have.

Cynthia's lips became pursed. So that was all he had to say about that!? Maybe he wasn't the sensitive and caring individual she thought he was?

"You're from hell!" she said spitefully to him.

McElroy lashed back at her quickly. "Yes. I have been there."

What was that telling her about him. Did he have an answer for everything? Just what kind of a man was this Robin McElroy. She hesitated. Maybe she hadn't known him long enough to lay all this heavy material upon him? That was it! Give it some time. She'd weave her way into his life yet.

The drone of music coming from his radio could be heard across the room. It wasn't playing loud enough to be recognized.

"I think you'd better go now," he told her. "This conversation seems to be going nowhere, if you know what I mean?"

"I think I do," Cynthia replied. "But you haven't heard the last of me!"

She took long strides across his room and out his hotel door. She did that without even saying "good-bye." This fellow did have a little "pizzazz," didn't he? He was "catchy." He was a new "toy" for Cynthia Craig to play with.

Chapter Ten

"It's Number One this week on Chicago's Big 96, WZMX," Travis Rinehart, the early evening disc-jockey on that station announced over the portable radio in Robin's room. "'Billie Jean', by Michael Jackson at The Big 96...."

McElroy was lying in the enormous, old-fashioned bathtub in his hotel room. The lukewarm water in it was up to his neck. The water was a milky hue due to the soap he was using to scrub himself. He wiped his hands with a towel and reached over the edge for a cigarette from his pack on the floor. The steel lighter he carried was next to the pack. He lit up the smoke and continued to lounge in that trough of a tub.

"Billie Jean" was a long number, and it had been on top of the hit parade for the past five weeks. While Michael Jackson's young voice was singing over the radio, Robin puffed on his cigarette in the tub.

"It's a boring life," he mumbled to himself. "And I like nothing more than to be bored with myself," he added.

His cross necklace was still on him while he bathed. Nobody could take that cross necklace away from him. Nobody. He pinched the gold cross between his fingers while he bathed and smoked. Robin studied it in its pristine beauty. That cross was all he had left now from Mary LaTella. It was a priceless memento of a more innocent time in his life. It also represented the only idol he now had. Jesus Christ.

He extinguished the cigarette in the lukewarm water when it burned close to the filter. "Billie Jean" was still playing in the other room. The day was Tuesday. Yesterday Cynthia had left his room in a bit of a tizzy. Today she had not yet dropped by. Maybe Robin had "snuffed out the fire" already? He'd nipped it in the bud? He'd guided his ship into fresh water and she had plopped to the river bottom? He didn't know what to think of that funny little girl. Mary LaTella stood for something. Cynthia Craig seemed to only stand for being some kind of a pain in the ass. There was a world of difference between the two of them. What a "mish-mash" of brains this brown-haired girl with the reddish tinge seemed to have. There just didn't seem to be a lick of sense to her at all. Money. His money looked good to her. The sooner she could dip her hand into his pocketbook, the better. That's what she was thinking. And in retrospect, how unselfish and caring that love from Mary LaTella had been. There was simply no comparison between the two of them.

While "Billie Jean" continued to play in his bedroom, recollections of some of the things Cynthia had already said to him were being focused in his mind's eye.

From the middle of the stairway towards the second floor, he recalled looking down upon her while she was asking the question.

"What does a girl have to do to get together with you?"

His mind flashed to yet another instance with Cynthia Craig. She was seated upon the bed in his hotel room. She was saying, "Really. I don't have enough money to live anyplace better. This place will do. I'm surviving."

"Billie Jean" was still playing on the radio in Robin's bedroom on Chicago's Big 96, WZMX.

He saw a mirage of Cynthia again, just the day before talking to him from beside his dresser.

"You're from hell!"

When McElroy heard her speaking that to him again, seeing the contorted look of anger crossing her face when she said that, he awoke. What in blazes am I doing with this woman? Is she out of my life now? She certainly has been interfering with my "karma."

The song finally ended. Travis Rinehart's voice came on over the again.

"Now it's time for WZMX News."

The radio station's "news sounder" echoed over the air, then a woman news reporter's voice came on the set.

"A new record was set today in Chicago while eighty-two percent of Chicago's 1.6 million registered voters turned out to participate in one of the most fervid campaigns ever staged in the Windy City. The result? Chicago has its first black mayor in Harold Washington while he defeated Bernard Epton by a narrow margin of 51 percent. Surprisingly, more whites voted for Washington than blacks who voted for Epton. Harold Washington told his supporters after the votes had been counted, 'We have finished our course and we have kept faith.'

"There will be more news after this message…."

Robin pulled the black plug on the drain with his big toe, and the bathwater slowly began to get sucked down that hole. He wouldn't have been surprised if the hotel was still utilizing its original plumbing system. He stood up and stepped over the top of the tub, then began to wipe himself dry with a towel he had purchased shortly after he'd moved into the hotel.

Upon entering his bedroom, he shut off the radio. He was sick of it. So what if Chicago has a black mayor? What was going on in the "rat race" outdoors really could've mattered less to Robin McElroy. He was "free" and flying over the sea without a destination.

While slipping into his undershorts, there was a knock at his bedroom door. Who else could it be. "I'm not decent," he told her.

"I'll be back later, then," Cynthia told him through the door.

McElroy listened to her footsteps walk away. He could hear them now because the radio was off. He could hear her door opening next door, then close behind her. What a pest!

Chapter Eleven

In Chicago, for Robin McElroy, on that same Tuesday evening, it was "All Quiet on the Eastern Front." Or was it? After he was fully dressed, he put on his black leather jacket and left the room. He filed down the staircase, through the dark hallway and out onto the sidewalk parallel to the street he lived on.

The sun had already set, but the days were getting longer. He was planning to have dinner at Rubin Paccino's Italian Café. Within seconds after moving along the sidewalk at a casual saunter, several feet away from the sign that read "The Saint James Hotel," five young men flamboyantly dressed emerged from the park across the street. They dashed across the street towards McElroy, then surrounded him. The gang's leader—wearing a tooth necklace, a circular gold earring in each ear, a mohawk haircut, and a brown vest with all kinds of strange etchings on it—began to talk to him. He hopped up and down upon his feet while he was walking around him. Was he on drugs? That was the first impression Robin got.

"You wouldn't want to cause us any trouble, would you?" the gang leader asked with a big white-toothed devilish grin. "I don't want to hurt you," another member of the gang added from behind The New Lone Ranger.

"All we want is your wallet," the leader explained.

"In fact, we'll even give you your wallet back. All we want is the money in it." The gang leader smiled dangerously at him again. "Now, you're not going to give us any problem about that, are you?" His eyes lit up daringly when he spoke the last sentence. The leader then produced a switchblade and pointed it at Robin's chin. "The wallet?" he asked again.

The leader of the gang was a black man. Robin knew this guy could split his gut in a moment's hesitation without feeling one iota of remorse. He was simply another animal living in the jungle.

McElroy's mind was suddenly thrust into a turmoil.

He showed no change of facial expression. He remained stone-faced throughout all this sudden onslaught of great pressure and crisis. His wallet contained six $50 bills. Should he let them have it? He had plenty more money back in his hotel room. Suppose they took his wallet anyway? Then there would be a problem.

"What's the matter?" the gang leader asked him in quick, biting manner. "Are you afraid of this knife? Wait till you see how you bleed when it cuts you open!" Robin groped to the Lord for an answer to these guys. He figured he'd probably be less the wallet too, anyway. They were all standing around him now, beaming at him with wolfish, bloodthirsty grins. They were all animals!

"The wallet?" the leader asked again, still bouncing up and down on top of his feet.

"I've got a problem," Robin suddenly protested.

"What's that!" the leader asked quickly. His eyes were now aflame. The switchblade became aimed at his abdomen. He was losing his patience with this McElroy.

The New Lone Ranger groped for more to say from The Lord. What could he say? These guys were suited up like clowns. That was it!

"Can I have this dance?" Robin asked.

"Dance!? What dance?" the leader asked him in a startled manner. He couldn't believe this man was denying him his wallet at knifepoint!

"Well…" McElroy said slowly, "it means I love you!"

The gang leader grimaced! Ew! A disgusting faggot! How the hell had they landed upon someone like that!?

"This guy's a fruit! Ha!" the leader laughed. "We don't want your money. But you will give us all blow jobs the next time we need them," he added.

Robin's stomach turned. He couldn't now believe that he had said that!

"Bye, Pretty Boy!" one of the gang members called back to McElroy while the "fearsome fivesome" bolted into the darkness of Manteno Park once again.

When Robin rounded the corner onto the sidewalk parallel to Halsted Street, he grinned to himself and let out a sigh of relief. Most likely he would never see those guys again. "Thank you, God," was all he said.

Chapter Twelve

About an hour after Robin had that most discomforting interlude with the street gang, he was finishing a ravioli dinner at Rubin Paccino's Italian Café. The waitress with the purple lips was working on the night shift now. Robin found out she did have a boyfriend, but apparently he wasn't the marrying type. At least he wasn't the marrying type for her. She was somewhat bizarre. Maybe that's what the problem with her was.

"Was your dinner all right?" she asked McElroy while handing him the bill.

"Good as it always is here," he replied.

She smiled, then bit her lip slightly. She knew he was unemployed. He'd told her he'd received a great amount of money through an inheritance. As a result of that, he didn't see any need to work.

"My boyfriend and I got into another fight last night," she told him. She was always telling Robin about all the fights she and her boyfriend had all the time. McElroy certainly didn't want to take stock in a woman who fought all the time.

"Your fault or his?" The New Lone Ranger inquired.

"His, of course," she said. "He's such a 'couch potato' who thinks he rules the world."

"I'm a 'couch potato' too," Robin added.

"Yeah," the waitress protested, "But you've got money. My boyfriend even makes me pay the rent."

"I'm sorry," he said. He didn't really mean it.

This girl, just like Cynthia, was trying to find a suitable angle to weave her way into his life. It's not easy being a ladies' man.

"I'm off work at eleven if you want to see me," she put in.

"My next door neighbor is coming over after I get back," Robin lied. "I did make her a promise."

"Well," the waitress added. "If you ever get tired of seeing her, you know where I can be found."

"Yes. I know. Can I have the bill, please?"

The waitress fidgeted through her apron for Robin's bill. She was a bit flustered that she couldn't make any headway with this prize.

"Here you are," she told him, extending the slip of paper with bill on it and adding a smile. "Come again."

McElroy whisked up the slip of paper and turned around, then strolled over to the cashier. It was a skinny man with black-rimmed glasses standing about six feet tall. His hair was dark brown and cut in a conventional fashion.

"How was everything tonight, Mr. McElroy?" the cashier asked.

"Just fine" was the quick reply.

The man rang up his bill and returned his change. After gathering up his coins and bills, Robin passed through the revolving door out onto the street. He wasn't walking down the avenue for more than thirty seconds when a blue and white squad car with a bright gold badge on the side of it coming his way slowed down and parked alongside the curb. There were two policemen in the automobile. The cop on the passenger side rolled down his window and called to McElroy.

"Where are you going?"

Robin turned to look at the round-faced patrolman with a ruddy complexion. He was wearing a blue visored cap and a dignified navy blue uniform. What did he want? The New Lone Ranger had figured by now that it was "cool" in Chicago. The thought that he was still a fugitive had been almost blocked out of his mind lately. Now, here, at this moment he was being confronted with a dilemma that could change the course of his life. He had to act fast. He put himself on the defensive immediately.

"The Saint James Hotel."

"Is that where you live?" the officer immediately asked.

"Yes," McElroy replied. Now was the time to lay the wood to them. If they had a warrant for his arrest, they were going to bust him now anyways.

If they didn't, he had a chance now to "bust their chops." "Now, I'd like to know what's going on here?" Robin quickly asked. "I haven't done anything wrong. If you boys are playing some kind of game with me," he said at the parked squad car, "I intend to call my lawyer and sue you both frontwards, backwards and upside down. Harassment. False Arrest. Should I try to think of some more?"

The officer with the ruddy complexion looked in upon the driver of the patrol car, who had also been listening to what The New Lone Ranger had been saying.

"That guy's all right," he could hear the driver say to his partner from the sidewalk.

"Sorry to have bothered you," the officer with the ruddy complexion called out the window to McElroy.

The driver of the patrol car put the vehicle into gear and with a more than average amount of acceleration, returned to traveling west on the street Rubin Paccino's Italian Café was located on.

If Robin McElroy was a fool for anybody but God, it had yet to be seen.

Chapter Thirteen

Memories of Mary LaTella came to mind again one morning in April while coffee was perking in the percolator atop his chest of drawers. He decided to blow off breakfast at Rubin Paccino's Italian Café and just have coffee on this morning. For lunch there were cold-cuts in the refrigerator. A jar of mayonnaise was now in there too. The orange juice was gone. He had a bottle of fruit juice and a half gallon of milk on supply.

Mary LaTella lived in a home that was "spanking neat." There was nothing shabby about that woman. She was by no means a "flake." Now. Does this Cynthia bear any comparison to Mary? He hadn't even seen her apartment yet. Suppose it was a pig-sty? Miss Craig was already showing signs of "irregularity" in character; fickleness. Could he deal with that? Did he want to deal with that? LaTella was always on the level with him except in "games." The games were all right with Robin. Was Cynthia playing games with him, or was her being a pain in the ass her being "straightforward" with him? There's a big difference between the games attitude and the straightforward attitude. If she was just playing games with him, he could "laugh off" some of the things he remembered her saying which got under his skin, such as "You're from hell!" And "You haven't heard the last of me!"

If she was serious, this really was a girl he didn't want any part of.

Robin could see Mary again in his mind's eye now. Her long, dark brown hair. That pink beret. Her tall, slender figure. She was wearing a white blouse bearing a gold necklace with a smaller cross than his own suspended from it. He could see her talking to him. Mary was a "perfect" woman, to him. Here she took this eighteen-year-old who was still a boy in 1968, and by the time he was twenty-one, she had made a man out of him. A good man. She had cultivated him with her own unselfish ways and in turn had created a man who was a "magnet" to all women. It was a slow, gradual procedure, but she did it. She took her sweet time teaching him this and teaching him that. By the time he was twenty-one, he was looking at the world the way all men really should, Every boy should have a "mother figure" just like Mary LaTella. She made him feel good about himself; she helped him find himself. She taught him to strive for independence. She once told Robin, "A man is a person who makes decisions for himself. He doesn't need anybody to tell him what to do. And he's not afraid to walk alone."

Those were the exact words Mary planted in his brain. She'd told him those words a couple of times. He would always remember them. He was a man now. He'd known the "real" acceptance by a woman. He now believed that few other men, in their quest to get into their girlfriend's pants, ever take the time to find out what really makes a woman tick. Robin knew now. There are certain things about most women that are "universal."

The coffee had finished perking. McElroy poured himself a cup. The cups he used were aqua-blue plastic coffee cups. He now owned four of them. Of course, most of this paraphernalia he'd recently acquired in town would be left behind if he decided to "bolt" for reasons beyond his control. At the time, though, this equipment was, indeed, functional and useful to him on a temporary basis. Steam drifted from the dark brown, almost black liquid in the aqua-blue-colored cup. He sipped it, gently.

He knew his "friend" Cynthia wouldn't be over to bother him until later. Today was another workday for her. No doubt she too had a cup of coffee at her desk in the Beacon Furniture Manufacturing Company on Chicago's South Side, where she was either typing something or receiving a telephone call. And "slaving" as she had once told him for her "hardnosed boss." Robin didn't feel sorry for her. She hadn't reached a soft spot with him yet. He didn't even like her that much.

She was a leech! What she wants is a husband, he thought, to "pay the freight" and give her support.

"1 should know that by now," he said out loud to himself. His mind was meandering with Cynthia now, imagining he could see her at work at her desk at the furniture company. He was seeing her through "God's Eyes" taking telephone calls and typing at her desk, while occasionally her "ugly" boss would come around and see what kind of progress he could make at either "belittling" her or "pronging" her.

No. The psychology of a woman was not strange to Robin McElroy. Apparently, now, he was her "light and ginger" at the end of a day; but for what reasons? At this point in time he could detect no vibrations of real love. Maybe it was too early. He had only known her on a regular basis for two weeks. Robin believed he could see through anybody, but the more he saw of Cynthia, the less lucid many of his theories had become. She was starting to become a mystery.

McElroy torched a cigarette to go with his morning coffee. The smoke wafted from its tip and diffused at the ceiling.

He could see Mary in the back of his mind once again while he smoked that cigarette. She was wearing a light blue winter sweater, the same gold cross necklace he'd seen her in wearing the white blouse a few minutes before. There was a small, aqua-blue-colored beret in her dark brown hair. She was talking to him again.

"In smoking, you're damaging the Temple of God. Your body is God's Temple. If you smoke, yes, you are sinning."

Under those circumstances, drinking and using drugs would also have to be considered a "sin." With those vices, as well, you're damaging the Temple of God.

"I don't drink or smoke dope," Robin reminded her back.

Mary looked down from him for a moment, then gazed back up into his young eyes.

"At least you're not the ultimate sinner, then," she informed him.

While Robin was still sipping on his coffee and puffing on his smoke, once again removed from "dreamland," he could hear noise coming from the east side of him; Room Number 22. It was another senseless tooth-and-nail argument going on between the couple that resided there. Not a day passed that they didn't argue at some time. Was he working? Robin didn't know. He had never taken the time to get to know them. He didn't want to take the time to get to know them. When they weren't arguing, he couldn't hear them. He could hear the sound of coitus coming from that room occasionally at night. She would moan, and he would pant loudly. After they had sex, they'd often argue. Robin really wondered how two people could go on living that way.

McElroy drained his cup of coffee and refilled it. There was now a slight queasiness in his stomach. He surmised it was the effect of coffee on an empty stomach. He looked at his wristwatch. Twelve noon was still a couple hours away. He reached atop his dresser and started munching on a slice of bread from the loaf he kept up there. It was soft, and wholesome. Once again, his mind "wafted off into The Land of Nod."

He could see himself breaking bread at church when he was a young man. Mary LaTella was seated next to him on the pew. It had been many years, now, since Robin had attended a church service. He recalled Mary seated next to him in her "spring green" dress; he was wearing a very light shade of gray suitcoat.

"So long as someone truly believes in Christ, he's granted eternal life in heaven," Mary was whispering to young McElroy. They were both wearing their cross necklaces. "There are many people who go to church and don't really believe. They go to church all their lives, but they're just going through the motions, following the crowd and not taking their acceptance of Christ seriously. The end result for those who don't believe, even if they do go to church, is hell after death."

Robin once again re-awoke from "dreamland." He knelt down upon his mattress and peered through his window. A car was passing by on the street below. There was an old man seated on Robin's green bench out in Manteno Park now. He was wearing a tacky old brown suitcoat and slacks; he had a brown cane looped over the top of the bench. His legs were crossed. He was just watching the world go by, the same way Robin did when he was out there.

The sun was beating down out there. It was warming up in Chicago. McElroy opened the window to let in some fresh air. Spring was now in its full form. At that moment, Robin suddenly felt captivated in this dingy little room. He climbed to his feet and decided to venture the great outdoors. When he exited the room, he always locked the door behind him.

In retrospect, Robin thought while he walked through the second floor hallway, Mary LaTella came around at a time in his life when it was easy for him to fall in love. With women coast-to-coast now acting like "drunken sailors" in his presence, it was really very hard for him to feel anything for any of them.

Chapter Fourteen

When he walked under the sign that read "The Saint James Hotel" within the same minute that he had left his room, he turned his head up and looked it over. It loomed in its luminescent state above his head. Its white light poured through the holes in it. Its yellow background with red letters radiated a different type of shade of light in the daylight. What a fine name for a hotel, Robin thought. He strolled across the street, which at this time was void of traffic, and entered Manteno Park. He started down the sidewalk which passed through the perk and looked all around him. The park was alive with verdant plant life. The air around him carried the stench of sulfur and other noxious elements. Despite this miscarriage of nature, the plant life endured. While passing by his green park bench which was still occupied by the old man in the brown suitcoat and slacks, Robin turned to look at him and asked the elderly gentleman.

"How are you?"

The old man kept on staring straight ahead. He ignored him. Either he wasn't playing with a full deck of cards, McElroy thought, or else life hadn't dealt him a very good hand.

The graffiti left behind by The Sheiks still littered the park. A new defacement in black spray paint had been added to the itinerary the night before. It was a positive form of defacement, nonetheless, according to Robin McElroy. The two words were: "Trust Jesus."

Looking straight ahead, he could see that building under construction south of the park. The men with the brown suits and scarlet-colored helmets were at it again. A jackhammer rattled like machine-gun fire on the concrete.

When the jackhammer wasn't operating, grating voices could be heard. Profanity. Abrasion. Dissention. Two welding torches glowed on the second floor of the structure against the steel girders. Their bright white light was emitted from flame-tipped torches held by men wearing gray masks. A fire of burning debris could be seen burning in front of the building. Its black smoke belched into the dirty blue Chicago skyline. Red and yellow flames licked the garbage. And there Robin was, walking through Manteno Park on what he may have called "The Avenue of Life."

When McElroy passed a statue in the park, while still hiking along that sidewalk, he noticed a man wearing white slacks and a blue denim jacket. The man was wearing very dark sunglasses. He was on his knees in the green grass holding a coffee cup in front of him with coins and a couple of dollar bills inside of it. When he heard Robin's footsteps coming on the sidewalk in front of him, the man said to him, not exactly looking his way.

"I'm blind. I need money."

The idea of having lost his own eyesight came to Robin. If he did, he would be doing exactly the same thing. The idea of being homeless and helplessly blind permeated his train of thought. What a travesty that would have to be! Robin thanked his lucky stars for what he had, even if it wasn't as much as many men in this country have and take for granted. He said a quick "Thank you" to the Lord for having preserved his own eyesight all these years, then thought about that man again. The Christian thing to do was to give him some money. But how much? McElroy stopped, opened his wallet, and looked inside. There were some ones, a five, two tens, a twenty, and five fifty dollar bills. Feeling a sudden onslaught of sorrow for this poor, helpless man, Robin plucked three fifty-dollar bills out of his wallet and deposited them into his coffee cup. He did not tell the blind man how much he gave him.

"There you go," Robin said to him softly. "Have a nice day."

"Thank you sir, thank you," the blind man replied. It could've been only a dollar bill he'd handed to this poor man, and he wouldn't have known the difference. It gave Robin McElroy an. overwhelming feeling of pleasure to know that that blind man could buy lunch at a McDonald's that day, and get about $147 back in change. Seeing that doing something of nature pleased The New Lone Ranger so. It would have to be said that he was, indeed, some kind of a saint.

Chapter Fifteen

April was drawing to a close now. There was a knock on Robin's door in the late afternoon one day.

"Come in, Cynthia," he said. "The door's unlocked."

She twisted the rattletrap doorknob and opened the door, then moseyed her way into his room. Seeing that McElroy was lying on top of his mattress, she found herself a place to stand next to his chest of drawers. The radio was not on. He was just lying on that bed puffing away on a cigarette and staring at the ceiling.

"You shouldn't smoke in bed," she cautioned.

"It's my room. I'll do what I want," he quickly replied.

"How are you today?" she asked pleasantly, yet in a spacey tone of voice. Her dilated brown eyes began to stare a hole in him. Robin hadn't yet taken notice.

"There's some coffee in the percolator," he offered, ignoring her question.

Cynthia opened the top dresser drawer, removed an aqua-colored coffee cup and tipped the percolator to fill it.

"How long has it been in here?" she asked.

"Since this morning."

"Ew," she told him. "I don't know if I want it then."

"I thought the coffee where you worked could clean a radiator," Robin protested. He became a bit irked that she had no grounds for many of the statements she made. At one time she would feel this way about something, and at another time she would another way about something. "First you tell me one thing, then you tell me another. Don't you think it's about time you got your shit together on how you feel about things?"

Cynthia had no answer to his question. She continued to stare at him while he lay atop his bed. She became at a loss for words through the coarseness of his speech. She was thinking, these daily visits rarely brought anything new. She didn't seem to be making any headway with this man regarding a relationship. This peeved her. She couldn't find an answer for the reason it was always her coming over to his room to visit. He never came over to visit her.

Her head, right now, was in a cloud. Miss Craig was in outer space. Her brown eyes continued to gaze upon that figure of manhood resting on the bed. He looked over at her, then blew a puff of smoke at the ceiling.

When he noted her vacant stare at him, he grimaced. He looked away from her, comprehending the vacant look in her eyes. When he shifted his glance her way one more time, he could see that she was still staring a hole through him.

"Are you high?" Robin asked her in an attempt to startle her. He knew getting high was her "Achilles Heel."

She turned her look away from him. Her lips pursed and began to quiver. She still kept looking away from him. She stared at the east wall of the room.

"Yeah," she finally confessed.

"Why do you come to visit me when you're high? We've really got nothing to talk about when you're like this." His words iced through her abdomen. It left her with an overwhelming feeling of guilt.

"I'm sorry," she said. "Are you sure you wouldn't like to toot some coke?"

"Knock it off! Why don't you just go back to your bedroom and sleep it off? I really don't like you around me when you're like this. You're creepy."

"I don't mean to be," she tried to explain.

"Where do you get that crap, anyway?" Robin asked.

"From a couple of guys named Rat and Ike. They toot it too."

It sounded to Robin that in her telling him that her so-called friends Rat and Ike tooted, that it was all right for her to toot too. She thought she was giving herself justification, then. To Robin, her rationale sounded just like sheer tomfoolery.

"Well, why don't you just tell Rat and Ike to stop delivery to your house? It's no wonder you can't afford to live anywhere else."

"But they're my friends," she told him spacily.

"With friends like that," Robin snapped to quote an old cliché, "who needs enemies!?"

"You really know how to hurt a girl," Cynthia complained. "Right now you're treating me just like garbage."

It appeared to Robin that she was trying to feel for a soft spot in him now. For her, there was no soft spot. There was still no feeling for her after several weeks of constant interaction. Would there ever be?

"Will you go back to your room and sleep it off? I'll talk to you later. Good-bye."

Positively, Robin thought, that was the best he could do for her. She needed to told to do things just like a child.

Cynthia stood up, leaving her full cup of coffee on the chest of drawers, then started out the door.

"You're mean, too." she added, weakly, while opening the door. She hesitated at the door, then looked back at him one more time.

"Go to bed." McElroy told her while watching her leave.

She entered the hallway and closed the door behind her. In the state of mind she was in, she didn't feel really hurt. Cynthia felt as if he just didn't like her. Maybe she should never come back to see him again? He was a bastard! He has one friend in the whole world, she thought, and he has to close the door on her. Why was he shutting her out? It wasn't because she was high, she decided. She was never going to succeed in "turning him on" to cocaine. He was too "square" for that. Why did she want to associate with a "square," anyways? He's just got some kind of problem he can't deal with, she assumed.

Where did he get all that money anyway? He must be some kind of a crook. Maybe she should report him to the police and have them conduct an investigation on him? Could they prove anything? They could ask him some questions. They could give him a lie detector test. That would be a nasty thing to do. Maybe it would be a good thing to do? Maybe he needed it?

She thought again. No. If she was into cocaine, they might find out what was going on with her. He could lash back at her and report that. That would be bad if she had the police up to his hotel room and they just happened to notice she was high.

Reporting him to the police would not be a good idea, she concluded. What should she do to him? Robin was the man she wanted. She'd already decided that. She had an inkling of that the first day she talked to him. But now, now this thing was probably never going to work out.

"I have to think of something," she whispered to herself while opening her bedroom door.

McElroy was thinking to himself, too, at this time. This woman is a real dud. She might have potential if she didn't use cocaine. She could even possibly be a bright spot in his life. Maybe he would even fall in love again? Who knows? She's so "girlish," he thought. Those freckles and all; she acts like a teenager, even though she's almost ten years older.

Cynthia never smiles when she's high, Robin noticed. She just bears that dumbfounded look across her face. Her eyes just "stare a hole through him." And when she's straight, those eyes suddenly come to life. She can be effervescent. It's the same difference between night and day. He was never going to fall in love with her, no matter how hard he tried, because she was so inconsistent. He was never able to predict what she was going to say or do next. Was that an asset? Did it make her interesting? No. It was a liability because when she was high, she just acted like a "space cadet" who knows nothing. When she was high, she was a "drag" to be with. And this altered state of awareness was occurring too often.

Robin figured he'd better have a good, long talk with her before writing off their friendship. He had to hand it to her, she was trying. She was giving it her all. Every day she was in his room. And he didn't even have to give anything back. As a matter of fact, this was the fourth or fifth time he'd turned her away. The reason was always the same when he turned her away, and there was no other reason he would turn her away for other than that. When she was straight, she was full of pep and a delight to be with.

Chapter Sixteen

On May 1, there was a knock at Robin's door earlier than expected that day. When he answered it, a deliveryman was standing in the hallway holding a basket with one white and two red roses in it. He said as soon as the door was opened, "A delivery for Robin McElroy. Are you Mr. McElroy?"

"Yes."

"Please sign here."

The deliveryman held out an invoice that needed to be signed by the receiver.

"Where did these flowers come from?" McElroy asked.

The florist glanced upon the tag tied to the basket and said.

"Cynthia Craig."

Cynthia. And, of course, it was May Day. Robin took hold of his ballpoint pen and signed the invoice, then told the deliveryman.

"Thank you."

He took hold of the basket and placed it atop his chest of drawers next to the percolator, then closed his bedroom door. He thought about her. Cynthia was thoughtful. It was time again, he decided, to weigh out the assets and liabilities of their friendship. He thought for a moment. It was as lucid as the sun is bright that she was giving this thing a try. A noble try at that. But what about her handicap? Could he live with her cocaine addiction? She was so sweet, yet so spacey. Her intentions no longer appeared to be dubious. So he did have money; if she couldn't stand him she wouldn't be in his room every day. Or would she? Probably not. She even seemed to thrive on his being nasty to her.

In the past couple weeks some of the nice things she had said to him when she wasn't under the influence of cocaine seemed to be genuine. Things such as:

"I've never met a man like you before."

And, "You really seem to be somebody special."

And, "I look forward to seeing you at the end of every day."

And finally, "No matter whatever comes between us, can we always be friends?"

He could see an image of her freckled youthful-looking face saying these things to him in his mind. They sounded so sincere. Yet she was a very confused young lady.

Her statements and emotions were as unpredictable as weather. How she was going to act on the days she entered his room could be anticipated as well as a longshot horse taking the lead and victory in a horse race. Maybe she was some kind of "longshot horse" in the back of his mind? Only time could truly tell.

He could see her in his mind's eye once again, saying things she'd said once before.

"Right now you're treating me just like garbage." And, "Why are you so mean to me?"

And finally, "Are you sure you don't want to toot some coke?"

Her entire problem seemed to be centered around that one habit. If it weren't for the cocaine, he might even take her seriously. If it weren't for the cocaine, everything would most likely be "roses," just as he was looking at on top of his chest of drawers.

At about 5:30 that same afternoon, Cynthia came prancing into his room in bubbly spirits.

"Hi!" she exclaimed when he opened the door after she knocked.

"Hi," he replied. "How's my 'Little Miss Star Wars'?"

She smiled, regardless of his insult.

"Did you like the flowers?" was the first thing she said.

"They're great! You didn't have to do that," he told her pleasantly.

"Well," she hesitated. "It's May Day, you know."

It was obvious to Robin at this point in time she was not under the influence of anything. When she was like this, he was most receptive to her conversation.

"How was work?"

"I didn't work today," she quickly said. "It's Sunday! Don't you remember?"

"I lose track of the days when I live like this," Robin put in. "So what did you do with yourself today?"

"I went to the Field Museum with a friend from work."

"Oh."

"It was another woman, if that's what you were thinking," she added, her eyes flickered temporarily like a candle, and she smiled too. "Who's the spacey one now?" she chided teasingly, regarding his statement about losing track of the days.

"I'm not saying anything," he told her, adding a yawn. "I can tell you're straight today and I'm pleased. You're not 'hiding.'"

"Let's go to the park," she suggested.

"Across the street?" he inquired dumbly.

"Of course across the street." She smiled again.

It sounded to her as if he was now playing games with her, acting dumb like she did when she was all doped up. "All right," he said.

Robin slipped into his black leather jacket. Cynthia was already wearing her blue windbreaker. She followed him out the door, down the staircase, through the hallway and out to the sidewalk. She was like a puppy dog at his heels. They passed under the sign that read "The Saint James Hotel." Before crossing the street, he took her hand and the two of them proceeded into Manteno Park. They meandered along the sidewalk and Cynthia was still her cheerful self.

"It's breezy today," she commented. "It would be a good day to fly a kite."

"I thought people only did that in March," Robin replied.

"Oh, no. When I was a girl, I sometimes even used to fly a kite in June."

She cast her eyes upon him with enlightenment scrawled across her face. She was ready, prepared to delve into a topic which McElroy very much liked to avoid. Her curiosity on this topic, though, overwhelmed her.

"Really, where did you get all that money?" she asked.

Robin's heart sank. It was something he just did not want to talk about. He was wondering why she didn't get the hint that he didn't want to talk about it from past conversations.

"I won it. I won it in a sweepstakes."

"Somehow I just can't believe that," she needled. The New Lone Ranger was on the defensive now. She'd put him there.

"Do you think I stole it?" he challenged.

"I don't know," she said. "I don't know if you could do something like that. Somehow you don't seem like the type who would. But I just keep wondering."

"Believe me!" Robin snapped. "I won it in a sweepstakes. I'm set for life if I want to live poor."

"So because you won it, you're not going back to work?"

"That is correct," he told her. "I've paid my dues on the workforce forever."

McElroy began thinking while there was silence between them while they walked through the park. Yes. It was his money that this friendship was based on. She was a parasite. He also knew she liked him for who he was. It appeared to him to be a funny combination.

"Don't you think this friendship we have is sort of miniature golf?" he asked her out of the blue.

"What is that supposed to mean?" she asked back. "Is it because we're not having sex? Is that it?" she challenged in return. She still hadn't quite comprehended what his question was about. Miniature golf? Peanuts. It wasn't intimate enough for him. That's what she concluded the meaning of it was. Actually, it wasn't that at all, to Robin.

The meaning of what he said, seeing it had failed to penetrate her conscience, was that he thought the whole thing about her "tagging around" with him for his money was "rinky dink." He could tell she hadn't caught on. Thinking about it again, after hearing her say that, he thought maybe it wasn't his money at all, after all. Maybe she just liked him?

"No. It has nothing to do with sex. Just forget I even said it," he said.

"What did you mean by miniature golf?" she pried further.

"It was just a choice of words I used. It sort of sums up what the two of us have been all about over the past month."

"It takes time for a friendship to grow. I'm not in love and you're not in love. So we need some time. That's all. Yeah. If you want to look at it that way, yes, it is 'miniature golf'."

Robin hesitated. Maybe right then and there she had hit the nail upon the head. Time. That was what they really needed. Time would tell what this thing was really all about. He thought now he could be sure of that.

"Now you know what I'm talking about," he added.

She crinkled her brow with disconfirmation, then smiled slightly. He was a mystery, wasn't he?

McElroy removed a cigarette from the pack in the pocket of his coat, then torched it with his steel lighter.

"Why do you smoke so much?" Cynthia inquired. "You smoke too many cigarettes."

"I smoke to damage The Temple of God," he replied stupidly. To him, whether or not he smoked was none of her goddamn business.

"Someday those things are going to kill you," she added.

"Should I put in my two cents' worth about your cocaine habit right now?" Robin stabbed.

Cynthia's eyelids became temporarily flustered, and her mouth corners suddenly tightened. The effect of his biting words had succeeded in doing what they had intended to do.

"You leave me alone about that, and I'll leave you alone about your smoking," she concluded.

McElroy wasn't done with her yet!

"There's no comparison!" The New Lone Ranger roared. "You're a zombie when you come into my room stoned and I wouldn't doubt your 'coke' is going to kill you someday too!"

Miss Craig's eyelids flustered again in the same nervous and agitated way again. Her mouth corners didn't tighten again this time, though. Instead the middle of her mouth took the tight form of an "O."

"Look! Over there! Flowers!" She pointed her finger at the pair of tulips that had sprouted up next to a tree in the park. "They're beautiful!"

Robin reckoned her decision to change the subject was probably for the better. He sensed a mild form of dissention breeding between them while on the topics of smoking and cocaine. After noting her quick reversal of the conversation, he wasn't quite yet ready to play along with it. His "defense mechanism" was still on.

"I'd like to take these home with me," she suddenly said. "I think I'm going to pick them."

"Help yourself," McElroy said softly. With a little more "oomph" in his speech this time, he added, "Just don't let a police officer see you doing that. He'll most likely concoct some charge such as 'defacement.'"

Cynthia pretended she didn't actually hear him. She uprooted the tulips and stashed them away in the pocket of her blue windbreaker. The petals of the tulips protruded from her pocket. Once again she held his hand. They walked briskly along the sidewalk which carved through the center of Manteno Park. They were at the south end of the park now and viewing the building under construction.

"What are they building there?" she asked.

"I never could tell. They've never posted a sign as to what it is to be."

"The men working on it have the day off today," Cynthia noticed.

"I feel sorry for them," Robin added. "That's a rough life."

Miss Craig became slightly befuddled at his last statement. Sympathy for laboring men, she wondered? Why? Maybe it was because he'd been off the workforce for so long? He obviously wouldn't want to trade "shoes" with them. After thinking that, she felt that she was getting to know Robin McElroy just a little bit better. In reality, The New Lone Ranger couldn't have cared less about those men. He was deceptive. A scam. A hoax.

"They probably don't think it's a rough life," Cynthia put in. "They probably don't know any better. Probably that's all they know."

Robin thought for a moment now, after she'd said what she'd said. When Cynthia was so alert and pleasant as she was now, he enjoyed her company. It was just those other times he could not stand and would not tolerate.

While walking, they crossed over the graffiti about "the times of no dope." Cynthia just looked down at it, but didn't say anything. She knew now around Robin that was not a "cool" subject to speak about.

"We'll have to travel into the Loop to do some shopping some day," she suggested.

"I could handle that."

"This city is so big I can't believe it," she said.

"It's a good place to get lost in," Robin added. There was a double-meaning to what he had said, but he knew she would never catch it.

"Well. We've got two of us," Cynthia said out of the blue. "Do we need anybody else?"

"We sure don't," Robin replied. He was defending himself again. He was now thinking, with her this way, it was better than being all alone. The only problem with was that their friendship wasn't always on this pleasant level. She was fickle. Unpredictable.

He thought some more. If they were to marry, eventually there would be others in their life. It would be inevitable. Would that blow his cover as a fugitive? It might. People would be wondering why he wasn't working. If he was to even apply for work, his credibility would have to be checked. It wasn't there. References. Past employment. The whole picture would've been suspiciously shady. And, of course, Cynthia didn't know her boyfriend was a fugitive. How long could he keep that secret? Just how long?

No, he concluded. No. It never could be. Robin finally decided again that he was right in the beginning; he had better keep his distance from this girl.

"Are you ready to go back in?" Cynthia suddenly asked, jostling his brain clear out of dreamland. There had been a long period of silence between them.

"Yes," Robin replied, quickly.

Chapter Seventeen

"Overkill," by Men At Work, was playing on WZMX in Robin's bedroom. The song had made it into the Top Ten. McElroy was puffing on a cigarette on his bed. Coffee was perking atop his chest of drawers. The time was 8:43 on his wristwatch. He had already shaved, brushed his teeth, and washed his face. It was just another day in The Windy City.

When "Overkill" came to its conclusion, the voice of Jenny Bright said, "WZMX. It's 8:45 at Chicago's Big 96. Looking for a bargain? The best values in foods can be found at your neighborhood Fashley Food Store. Mouth-watering filet mignon is only $2.79 a pound this week at Fashley…Swiss Creme Soda, we're overstocked and six-packs in cans are going for the low, low price of just 69 cents. That's not the end of it! Fresh and tasty California Strawberries are now in season and are in abundance at the remarkable price of only 59 cents a pint. The sale is going on this week, so stock up on the super values Fashley Food Stores have always been known for. Fashley Food Store—where your shopping needs are our only concern."

The Fashley Food Store jingle followed the disc-jockey's announcement.

"Michael Mania is in full swing this year, fans!" Jenny Bright then announced. "Let's do it up with 'Beat it' on Chicago's Big 96…."

While the contemporary number "Beat It," by Michael Jackson, was playing on his radio, the coffee in Robin's percolator was ready. He removed one of the aqua-blue cups from his top dresser drawer and poured himself a cup. While sipping on the steamy-hot chocolate-colored fluid, he lit another cigarette and looked out the window. The sun was shining. The grass in Manteno Park was green and freshly cut. Leaves were growing on the trees. And to his left was the looming red and yellow neon sign that read "The Saint James Hotel."

McElroy noticed something had been eating out portions of his loaf of bread. The plastic had been gnawed away and bread crumbs littered the area around it in the dresser drawer. On this particular day, Robin spotted the culprit. He noticed a big rat scuttle across his floor from under the chest of drawers. The rat disappeared into a hole in the wall of the bathroom under the sink. A rat! He supposed it was to be expected in a dump like this one. This bread vandalism had been going on for quite some time. The New Lone Ranger decided to name his new "friend" Roger.

The disc-jockey's voice came over the radio again following the song "Beat It."

"Jenny Bright here on WZMX. I've got 68 at O'Hare. I've got 65 at the Lakefront and 69 at WZMX. Prepare for a beautiful spring day everybody! It's hot this week on Chicago's Big 96, here's Laura Branigan with 'Solitaire' on WZMX…."

Robin finished his cup of coffee. His stomach was telling him he needed food. Breakfast. He decided he'd go to Rubin Paccino's Italian Café for their breakfast special. He put on his red sweater, made sure his cross necklace was hanging outside of it, turned off the radio, and left his hotel room.

Chapter Eighteen

At Rubin Paccino's Italian Café, Robin ordered Special Number Two again from a medium-built black waitress. While seated at his stool at the counter, that familiar police officer entered the restaurant and sat down next to him. He was quiet, at first. The same black waitress then came to take his order.

"What'll it be today, Ollie?" she asked.

"Special Number Three, with a coffee and a small orange juice."

"Coming right up!" the waitress told him brightly.

The policeman turned to look at McElroy.

"Haven't I seen you in here before?" he inquired to Robin.

"I'm not sure," the fugitive lied.

"Ollie Winnowski."

The police officer then offered his hand. Robin shook it, with hesitance.

"I've seen you in here before," the officer added. "You eat at this place all the time."

"That…I do," McElroy stuttered.

"What do you do for a living?" the policeman asked.

Robin McElroy was beginning to feel as nervous as a turkey does in November. Suddenly he felt as if he was seated on a hot bed of coals.

"I'm unemployed," he replied quickly. His entire emotional level was now put completely on the defensive. He was not going to offer any information he didn't have to. With the pressure building up in him at a rapid rate, this bundle of nerves now was ready to burst at any moment. He felt as if he was being interrogated. Did this policeman really know anything about him? This had to be some kind of investigation, he thought. Robin was not the "big man" he was on that night the two "boys in blue" in the squad car tried to pry some information out of him. He was feeling smaller and more helpless by the second. What was Ollie's interest in him? The suspense was overwhelming.

"I've been on the beat here for twenty-three years," the policeman put in. "I'm sorry to see you're unemployed. Have you been looking for a job?"

"Every week," Robin spat out.

He was immersing himself in a pool of lies he would never be able to untangle if he ever got to know this man better. His right leg started shaking.

"Nervous?" the policeman asked, noticing his leg jiggling.

"I had too much coffee this morning," Robin lied again. "That caffeine gets me as high strung as a piano wire."

"Oh," the officer said. A look of skepticism suddenly crossed his face. He wasn't quite sure he was believing what he heard. There seemed to be something wrong with the picture Robin McElroy was painting. His twenty-three years of the force was telling him so.

"What's your name?" the cop asked. Ollie wanted to sink some kind of hook into this "fish" if he planned to land him some day. Knowing his name was a good way to lay a foundation for finding out more about him in the future.

"Robin McElroy."

No other name could reach the end of Robin's lips while being in the demoralized state he was now in.

"Well, Robin McElroy," the officer said. "There are a lot of jobs waiting out there if you look hard enough. I don't like to see anybody who can work unemployed."

McElroy swallowed hard. He dipped his fork into his eggs and almost dropped it. They had been served to him while Ollie and he had been having their talk. Their conversation had been uninterrupted by the black waitress. Robin knew after this encounter, if he ever made it out of this cafe without being arrested, he would certainly be under some kind of suspicion by this police officer. Then it was time to leave town, Robin thought.

"You don't say much, do you?" the policeman

"I was raised not to say much," McElroy lied again.

"That's a handicap in the big city," the policeman told him. "That could be the reason you haven't found a job yet. Talk at the interview. Don't be afraid to reveal yourself. You've got nothing to hide, do you?" the cop pried further.

This interrogation was sheer torture. Robin's thinking was scrambled beyond belief at this point. He just prepared himself to spew one lie after the next until he could get out of this place.

"I've got a clean record. Good worker," Robin put in.

"I hope the next time I come in here to see you, you're gainfully employed," the cop said to him.

"I do too," McElroy lied again. He was feeling invariably sheepish by this time. "It's tough. It's tough for me to find work anyways."

"Finding a job is what you make it," the officer explained to him confidently. "For one thing, you shouldn't be nervous when you talk to people. I've noticed that about you."

Robin dipped his fork into his hash browns. He wasn't going to be arrested, he thought. This cop had nothing on him. He was just feeling him out. There is no warrant, he concluded. There was nothing to be afraid of.

"You must like the food here," the cop said, changing the subject.

"It's the best. That's why I always come here." The fugitive was beginning to feel a little bit more relaxed with him now.

"Well, I'll tell you one thing," the officer said. "You're going to have to open up more if you want a job around here."

"I come from a small town out east," Robin lied again. "Living in Chicago is a big adjustment for me."

He suddenly felt that that last line was a good cover for himself.

"Let me tell you a secret," the officer put in. "In the city, it's every man for himself. Nobody really cares. I've worked this beat for twenty-three years. I know. Living in the city is a sink-or-swim situation. And believe me, a lot of people sink. Look at all the homeless people this city has."

"If that's what I notice starting to happen to me," Robin told him, "then I'll get out."

"You'd better," the officer warned him. His words this time were like a spade being driven into a bed of gravel.

After making that statement, the officer became preoccupied with his meal which had just been served. He'd had his word with this "mouse." Robin ate his breakfast as fast as he could. He wanted away from this policeman so, so bad. Right now he had to be suspect of something, he thought. His actions had been too conspicuous. His words and lies must've for certain sounded "faulty" to this veteran of twenty-three years on the beat. When Robin finished everything except for his biscuit, he said to the officer with a quaver in his voice, "It was nice to meet you."

"The next time I see you," the officer replied, looking up from his breakfast and into McElroy's eyes, "I want to know that you are gainfully employed."

"I hope so too," Robin lied again. "If not, I'll be out of town."

The quivering remained in his voice.

McElroy left three quarters on the counter for the waitress, then went to the cash register to pay for his breakfast.

"Was everything okay?" the heavy-set black woman cashier inquired.

"Just...fine...." Robin stuttered.

Again, no notice was taken of his uneasiness by the cashier. Her question was strictly mechanical. As were her actions.

When he exited through the revolving door, he couldn't believe he was finally out of that place! The pressure of it all was so overwhelming that he couldn't stop thinking about it for a couple hours after he was back in his hotel room.

Chapter Nineteen

When Cynthia came to visit later that day, Robin was still contemplating whether or not to leave Chicago. That officer's conversation with him that morning had left McElroy as tight as a drum. When he opened the door to let her in, Cynthia flung her arms around his neck and pressed her lips up against his. Her mouth opened slightly, and her tongue unleashed itself against his lips and teeth. She held her mouth against his for a long moment. Her tongue rolled around gently inside of his mouth, touching his tongue. They both closed their eyes and felt a first feeling of intimacy. It was a pleasant feeling to Robin, a feeling he had not known in a long period of time. He could feel her tongue penetrating, yet not "violating" his territory. It was slippery and wet. And intimate. When she moved her face back, Robin was able to talk and said in a deep voice.

"What's this all about?"

"I just thought I'd give you a 'big ole kiss' when I came to see you today," Cynthia explained. There was a flicker of rapture in her eyes.

McElroy noticed she was, indeed, straight today. He could always tell by her eyes. This afternoon her eyes were full of life.

"An intimate kiss at that," Robin added.

"One of us had to be the first to promote it," she said. "I'm not an iceberg, you know."

"I can see," McElroy replied.

"What's new with you?" Cynthia inquired, changing the subject.

"Nothing is ever new with me. You should know that by now," he told her. He was also lying. The idea of leaving Chicago for good was now heavy on his mind.

"I've got a week's vacation coming up in August," Miss Craig said to him. "What do you say we take a trip to Florida?"

"Florida?"

"Yes. Florida. Wouldn't that be a marvelous time?"

"Who's going to pay for it?" Robin challenged, knowing full well now it looked as if she was trying to dip her fingers into his pelf for the first time, and finding a way to knock him off guard with that flamboyant wet kiss.

"We'll go dutch. You don't have to worry about that," Cynthia explained.

McElroy hesitated. He may be long gone by August, he thought. He finally gave her a non-committal reply.

"Maybe."

"Maybe," she repeated. "Let's think seriously about it. I'll give you some time to think about it. I'd really like to go. It would give 'us' a chance to see each other in a different light. Do you know what I mean?"

"Yes, it would," Robin added.

It looked to The New Lone Ranger now that Cynthia was really ready to play "hardball." He knew in his own mind already that he was not ready for that. At least not with her. There were some things about her that he could not condone. Now he was in a pinch. So long as he lived at this residence, he was already too far involved to back out on her. Getting rid of her at this point in time would be an impossibility so long as he lived in The Saint James Hotel. Now the desire to vanish from this community was even getting stronger.

"You're 'spacing out' on me," Cynthia said.

"So I am. How was work?"

"No better today than yesterday," she replied. "That boss of mine is still a thorn in my side."

"And I'm sure he always will be," Robin added.

There was another moment of silence, then the effervescent Cynthia asked, "Can I have some coffee?"

"Help yourself."

McElroy thought of something to say. He then put in, "What's his name?"

Cynthia gave him a strange look after he said that he eats his bread. What on earth was that supposed to mean? She decided instead of making a big issue out of his probable play on words, she just decided to ask what his friend's name was.

"Roger."

"Roger who?"

"Roger the Rat," Robin said bluntly.

"Roger the Rat? What do you mean? Do you mean your friend is a rat!?"

"There's a rat living in this room in the hotel," McElroy finally explained.

Cynthia shrugged her shoulders after hearing him out. She shifted her glance away from him randomly towards the dormant charcoal-colored heating unit.

"I wouldn't doubt it. This place is such a dump."

Cynthia turned around and poured herself a cup of coffee. She sipped it from one of the aqua-blue coffee cups. At the same time, Robin ignited a cigarette.

"So there is something new with you," Cynthia put in.

"I suppose that is news."

"Seriously," Cynthia told him. "Think about going to Florida with me this August. I'd really love to go."

"We'll see. I'm not saying 'yes' or 'no' at this point in time."

"Look!" she exclaimed boldly. "You've got money coming out of your ears! You owe it to yourself if nobody else!"

"I don't want to talk about it anymore. Can we just put that subject away for now?"

"Think about it," she said one more time. "That's all I want you to do right now. Will you do that for me?" Her words were pressing.

"Okay," he replied, softly.

"This coffee tastes old," she complained.

"I put it on this morning."

"I'm going to dump it down the bathroom sink. It's no good," she told him.

Robin noted her pushiness today. And, of course, that vacation in Florida was where she was going to try to "tie the knot." He realized now he was getting himself into something he couldn't back out of. So long as he lived here, she was going through the motions to promote a marriage.

She had him picked out the first day. As soon as he told her he didn't have to work, she'd found herself just the right man to target. She liked him. True. But after knowing what real love was, between him and Mary, this just wasn't the same. He asked himself, could he live with her? No.

Cynthia had just dumped the old coffee down the sink in the bathroom. She called out to him from the bathroom.

"Can we go out to dinner tonight?"

"No," he quickly replied.

"Why not?" she asked.

She re-entered the bedroom and gazed upon him with her lively brown eyes. There's was a noticeable hint of insecurity written in them.

"Because I'm having dinner here tonight."

"I will join you," she said.

"Suit yourself. I'm having cold-cuts sandwiches."

"For dinner!? That's no kind of dinner for you," she told him. "What you need is woman around to see that you eat right."

"Will you go back to your room now?" Robin asked. "I've got a headache."

"You do?" It was the first time she'd ever heard that.

"Yes. I've got a headache." He was lying, but he was feeling some kind of sensation during this conversation that she was succeeding in tying his brains into some kind of a knot. "I'll talk to you again tomorrow."

He opened the door for her. Cynthia figured he was lying about the headache. It may have been a first time he used that excuse to get rid of her, but somehow she felt as if she was just not wanted because she had been alienating him with her pressured conversation. Through her eyes now it was do or die. She had to lay the wood to him sometime.

She quickly flashed back to his comment on "miniature golf." With that big wet kiss, had she finally gotten her little white ball on the first tee of a real golf course? She was still thinking that was what he had meant by that. As she walked out the door, she gave him a gentle peck on the cheek with her lips.

"Good-bye," she said softly, glancing into his eyes and then shifting away while she disappeared into the hallway.

She knew if she was going to corner this man, she had better not push too hard in the beginning. She'd struck with full force today. Now she reckoned it would be time to lay off for a while. He just might fly the coup. It would be better, she thought while opening the door to her room, to let him have his own way for a while, then force him to make a commitment later.

Chapter Twenty

One Saturday afternoon, late in May, Robin thought he heard a knock at his door. When he opened his door, there was nobody there. He just happened to look to his left out his door, and noticed two black men standing at Cynthia's door. One of them was wearing an ebony-colored derby hat, sunglasses, and gray coveralls. The other was wearing a maroon cap, sunglasses, an old gray suitcoat that was tattered, and a pair of matching gray slacks. They looked suspicious. Were these two Rat and Ike, the guys Cynthia told him she bought her cocaine from? Robin suspected they were. The two of them looked at McElroy after he opened his door, then looked back at Cynthia's door. Finally, Cynthia answered and he could hear her say to them, "Come in."

Before going through her doorway, the two of them looked over at Robin one more time. Very suspicious, McElroy thought. Cynthia closed the door behind them. Robin waited a moment, then tip-toed over to Cynthia's door to listen to what kind of talk was going on inside her room. He could hear them talking.

"Who's your neighbor?" one of the men asked.

"He's just a neighbor," Robin could hear Cynthia reply. "Don't worry about him."

"It's all there," the other man put in. "A quarter of an ounce."

"I don't have to test it out," Cynthia told them. "I know you guys wouldn't cheat me. Let me get you your money."

There was a long pause while Robin was listening. He was going to have a word with those pushers when they came out. Robin shifted his feet slightly outside of the door to Cynthia's room. Whether or not the pushers could hear that, he couldn't tell. He wanted the element of surprise to be on his side.

"Here's your money," he finally heard Cynthia say. "That last stuff you guys got me was excellent. I got lost in the painted sky on it."

"We deal with only the best," one of them boasted. "Give me a call when you run out," the other one added.

The door opened, and the suspicious pair exited into the hallway.

"What are you doing here!?" the one in the maroon cap asked of Robin angrily. It seemed in the way he said it that he already knew who he was.

"You wouldn't happen to be The Man?" the one in the black derby inquired.

"Listen up, you guys," Robin said in an authoritative voice. "I want you two to stop selling her dope. She's my friend, and I don't like to see her spending half her life acting like a zombie."

"Any friend of Cynthia's is a friend of mine," the one in the derby explained. "Let's teach this asshole a lesson!"

The man in the black derby slammed Robin against the wall in the hallway, then he removed a switchblade from his coveralls. He put the tip of the knife up against the inside of Robin's nose, then yanked it back out towards himself. The end of McElroy's nose was sliced open, and blood suddenly gushed over his lips and chin. The pain was not that bad initially.

After hearing some commotion in the hallway, Cynthia opened the door to her room and looked out. After seeing the blood pouring out of Robin's nose, she screamed!

"What are you guys doing!?"

"Personal business. Is this guy going to be a problem to us? If he is, I'll waste him right here."

"No! Not at all!" Cynthia exclaimed. "Let him be!"

"You're off the hook, asshole," the one in the maroon-colored cap said to Robin.

"Just don't let us see you hangin' around again when we're doing business with the lady," the one in the black derby told him.

His attacker let go of him, and the two ambulated off through the hallway and on down the staircase.

"I'm so sorry!" Cynthia exclaimed to Robin.

"What were you doing out here?"

Robin entered his room and ran some water in the sink on one of his towels. He held the towel up to his gaping wound. Blood was just trickling out of it now.

There was a smattering of blood all over the front of his cotton shirt. Now the wound was starting to sting.

"Let me get some iodine," Cynthia said.

She brought some iodine and a bandage into his room from her room. It seemed to Robin to be the first time she was ever really a help. His accident was on account of her anyway. When she applied the orange-colored healing solution to the wound, it burned immensely.

"Now can you tell me what you were doing out there?" Cynthia asked.

"I wanted to talk to those guys about selling you cocaine. I don't like it."

"Never interfere with Rat and Ike," she cautioned. "They're dealers and they're very paranoid. They probably thought you were a cop."

"I'll tell you one thing," Robin said. "Those two have not heard the last of me."

"I'm warning you," Cynthia said. "Leave those two alone. They can be very dangerous."

McElroy applied the bandage to his nose himself.

Blood was still seeping out of the wound. His nose felt as if it were on fire.

"They haven't heard the last of me." he repeated.

"I'm warning you," Cynthia told him. "They're not to be fooled around with. They could kill you! They might have killed you if I hadn't come around to talk them out there in the hall. They think nothing of killing people. If you violate their territory, you've had it!"

"I could kill them!" Robin burst out.

"What was your reason for listening in on them in the first place?" Cynthia asked. "You were only looking for trouble."

"Look. I don't like the effect cocaine has on you. I wanted them to stop selling it to you. I might even like you better if you cut out that crap!"

"Just leave all of us alone. It's not going to stop. Mind your own business from now on and you'll be all right."

Robin started thinking. She was placing the value of her cocaine habit above the value of him. It didn't matter what happened to him, or if their friendship really lasted, just so long as she had some coke to blow up her nose!

"That's easy for you to say. You're a zombie when I see you on that stuff. And it's their fault. And now look at what they've done to my nose! I'll probably be permanently disfigured. I should probably have stitches for it. Look! It's still bleeding! I could kill them! And you're still going to buy that shit that makes you act like Lurch!"

"Just settle down," Cynthia said soothingly.

She put her arms around him. He was her big baby now.

She began to caress his arms with her hands. "Just settle down and relax. Everything's going to be all right."

Chapter Twenty-One

Over the Memorial Day Weekend, Robin and Cynthia had purchased some swimsuits at a store in The Loop, and during the first week of June took the bus out to a beach on Lake Michigan.

"It's too cold to go swimming this early in the year," Cynthia complained, after having had dipped her feet into the sandy shallows.

There were a few people basking in the sun, and a few others were wading out into the water. The temperature was seventy on this weekday. Miss Craig had called into work "sick."

Robin started wading out into the rather cold waters of Lake Michigan. To get away from the dismal vicinity he lived in for a little while was a treat. He decided he was going to take full advantage of it. The brisk, wavy water erupted goosepimples all over his body.

It chilled him to the bone.

"It's too early to go swimming this time of year," Cynthia repeated, calling to him from her towel in the sand.

"I don't care," Robin called back. "How often do I get to go swimming, anyways?"

McElroy actually found the cold waters invigorating. He buried his body up to his neck under water. His teeth started to chatter. Chill blame. A lighthouse could be seen in the distance. White-capped waves beat against a nearby levy. There were a number of sailboats and speedboats out on the lake.

When Robin wasn't watching her, Cynthia turned her back to him, produced some tinfoil from her purse and rolled up a ten-dollar bill. She unfolded the foil which held within it a white powder. Through the rolled-up ten-dollar bill, she sucked up some of the powder through her nose. She looked back to see if Robin still wasn't watching her. He was looking at the lighthouse in the distance. Cynthia then re-wrapped the tinfoil and stashed it back in her purse. Before he came out of the water, she was already starting to feel the effects of the cocaine.

"I've had enough of that for the day," Robin said while shivering a few feet away from her. He dried himself off with his towel, then stretched the towel out on the sand and lay atop of it.

"Think it's a good day to get a tan?" he asked, gazing up at the almost perfectly blue sky.

She didn't answer him. She heard him, but she couldn't think of anything to say.

"I heard on the radio it's supposed to reach eighty today." McElroy told her.

Again. She said nothing.

"You're not saying much," he put in.

"I'm sorry," she replied.

McElroy watched the white-capped combers roll into the shore and dissolve upon the sand at the edge of the beach. Cynthia lay upon her stomach staring straight ahead at the parking lot opposite the lake from the beach. Her reticence became noticeable to Robin after he spoke again.

"We should come here once a week," he suggested. Again. There was silence coming from the party to his left.

"Are you all right?" he finally asked.

"Yes," was her spacey reply.

McElroy looked her over. She was wearing a yellow bikini, which housed some well-proportioned buttocks and breasts. Her heinie was round and caught the eye. Her hair had become tangled in the light breeze which swept over the beach. Her eyes! He took a good long look at her eyes! They were glassy and red!

"Are you high?" His words stabbed at her.

"No." She lied.

"I can tell you are," he put in. "I can see it in your eyes. Why did you have to do that on a nice day like this? Can't you enjoy some place of something without having to see it through a drug?"

"I'm sorry," she murmured.

Now she knew, without any further talk between them, that their day on the beach was ruined. He wouldn't forgive her for it. He was going to chew her out now. She knew that. She knew right now that the forecast was calling for "pain."

"I'm sorry," she repeated.

"All right," he said, trying to make a point. "Let's go home. I don't want to be around you when you're like this. We'll both go back to the hotel and you can sleep it off. It's the same thing we always do when you get this way. You know by now that I'm not going to put up with it. I don't enjoy talking to a wall, or someone with the intelligence of a wall when they're under the influence of cocaine. You really don't know how pathetic you are when you're stoned."

Tears began to well in her eyes. A single teardrop rolled down her left cheek. It streaked down her cheek and plopped on the towel below her.

"I'm sorry," she murmured again. A saliva bubble formed between her lips. Another teardrop rolled down her left cheek, then her right eye began to "shower" too.

"Someday you're going to learn that I'm not 'cool' to drugs. When you're off in another world, I don't care to be around you. If you want to destroy yourself, that's your own business. Just don't come calling to me when you're a basket case."

After hearing that, Cynthia burst fully into tears. His words were so firm and biting. He was a bastard!

"You're so nasty!" she complained, in defense of her weakness. "I just wanted to have a little fun."

"Have that kind of fun someplace else when you're not around me."

"You know, Robin McElroy," Miss Craig protested, "sometimes you're a real bastard."

Tears continued rolling down her cheeks, and she started sobbing to the point that she could no longer speak.

"Let's go home," he whispered, softly, yet firmly.

Chapter Twenty-Two

As the month of June progressed, during the day it often became uncomfortably warm in Robin's hotel room. Naturally, the hotel was not equipped with air-conditioning. One day, he purchased an oscillating fan from a drug store to help circulate the sultry air in his bedroom. This helped a little.

One morning the radio was going and Robin was in the bathroom shaving with his electric razor. Jenny Bright was the disc-jockey. "I've Got A Rock N' Roll Heart," by Eric Clapton, was playing on WZMX. The song had been off the Top 40 for over a month now, but Jenny Bright was still playing it. Robin had heard her once state on the air that she did, indeed, like Eric Clapton and wished he'd break into the Top 40 more often these days.

When he finished shaving his face, he looked in the mirror at his nose. There was a scar on it where the knife had cut through it. The skin had healed unevenly because it had never been stitched. That token of his encounter with Rat and Ike would be with him for the rest of his life. No. He would never forget those two.

He heated the water from both the hot and cold handles on the sink, in the sink, to the temperature that was correct to splash his face with While the water was spewing out of the spigots, he recollected a memory of Mary LaTella once more. She was wearing a lime-colored dress from her usual Marshall Fields, and dictating to him again in words he could not remember. He could just see her lips moving. The gist of this memory was established in the fact that after a couple of years of "pushing" and "shoving" between them, forceful blows being delivered from both sides in vehement conversation between the two of them, Mary LaTella had finally succeeded in making a "teddy bear" out of Robin McElroy. The end result of his correspondence with her was that The New Lone Ranger would never again be a "threat" to women. She'd cut his cock off! Robin rubbed the water over his face which was in the trough at the proper temperature now and splashed it until it was dripping wet then cleared off his visage with a towel.

Did his encounter with Ollie Winnowski the month before at Rubin Paccino's Italian Café stop him from going there again? No. Robin figured that police officer had no right to tell him he must work. That was Robin's own prerogative whether or not he wanted to work. He was cultivating his defense against Winnowski now. He figured this cop was just using his uniform as a device to belittle people. So long as McElroy was paying his bills, he could see no reason why he must be "gainfully employed" by the next time he spoke with Ollie Winnowski. That idea was now stuck in his head. The police officer was just an asshole who was trying to cast his dominance over the entire community because he was wearing a badge. True. He did deserve respect. But when he starts violating the territory of people for illegitimate reasons, then he's just being an asshole.

Chapter Twenty-Three

At Rubin Paccino's Italian Café later that morning, he did indeed meet up with Ollie Winnowski.

It was almost if by coincidence, seeing that he'd just been thinking about him that morning. The officer sat next to him while he was having his breakfast.

"How are things?" the policeman asked him. His was a tone of friendliness in his voice.

"Fine," Robin replied. "How are things with you?"

"I'm not complaining."

The same medium-built black waitress who'd taken both their orders during the previous interlude between them came to take the policeman's order.

"What'll it be, today, Ollie?" she asked with an air of cordiality.

"The usual," the officer replied. "Special Number Three."

"And that's with coffee and a small orange juice?" she asked.

"Right."

Robin was having his usual Special Number Two, and was in the midst of it when Ollie arrived at his side.

"Robin McElroy? Right?" the officer asked.

"That's my name," Robin lied.

"Have you found a job yet?"

"Still looking," McElroy quickly replied. "Now, so long as I'm paying the bills and not obtaining this money by illegal means, what's it to you?"

These words from The New Lone Ranger attacked the policeman like a snakebite. Suddenly he'd been kicked off this pedestal he'd placed himself on. He searched for an explanation for his badgering; one that was credible.

"Look!" Ollie exclaimed. "If you're not going to work in this community, I want you out! Is that understood? There is no place for slackers and bums on my beat!"

"Yes, sir," McElroy replied softly.

"I'm giving you one more week to find a job," the cop warned him in a grating voice. "One more week. You don't want to know what's going to happen to you if you don't obey my orders and I catch you in here again!"

"Yes, sir," Robin replied softly again. Verbally, he was bending over for authority.

McElroy was no longer afraid of him. It was obvious he had nothing on him. He gulped down the rest of his orange juice, then sipped on his coffee. This policeman was just a crusty old codger who got his kicks out of hassling "innocent" people. Innocent, to the best of Ollie's knowledge anyway. Here was a fugitive, Robin thought, "laughing" in the face of the police. What guts he had! Robin was proud of himself for taking a cut at this stuck on himself cop. He was quite proud. He just realized he'd better not push his luck any further, or old Ollie might be able to find some reason to take him "downtown." If he was ever booked by the police department, he was certain his past would surface and be revealed in full. If that was to happen, he would end up doing his time for the state. It would be a long time at that.

"If I don't have a job by next week," Robin added when he stood up after finishing his meal, "I will leave town as you requested." He was lying.

McElroy never saw Winnowski anyplace but at Rubin Paccino's Italian Café. Robin decided now that Rubin Paccino's Italian Café had just lost one of its best customers because some cop stepped out of his limits and alienated that customer.

"That's the spirit!" Ollie replied in a gruff voice.

At that Robin plinked some coins on the counter for a tip, then approached the cash register to pay his bill for the very last time.

While he passed through the revolving door, he thought of something he had wished to tell Ollie Winnowski, but knew it was not "cool" to say to him. Those words were: "It's not that painful…just a little degrading." But Robin was already certain in the first place that Ollie had no intentions of ever becoming his "friend."

Chapter Twenty-Four

By the last week of June, Robin was feeling serious about getting a "divorce" from this community he was now living in. That confrontation with Officer Winnowski was just about the straw that broke the camel's back. Not to mention the fact that the desperation in Cynthia was getting more and more apparent in her daily visits to his hotel room. There was no way he could marry her. His being a fugitive was reason enough not to condone any marriage. The other reason was her cocaine habit. When she was under the influence of that drug, he couldn't tolerate her. And she was now getting tough to deal with even at times when she was straight.

In preparation for his departure, Robin had another fake I.D. manufactured at a conspicuous spot on the South Side. He had a driver's license now that had his picture and the name Rodney Applegate on it. The illegal identification only cost him $25.

At nine o'clock one morning late in June, Robin already had his fan going, and of course, his radio was on. It was almost 80 degrees in his hotel room. He kept the window halfway open most of the time now. The sound of voices in the park or the drone of automobile, truck, or bus engines never ceased.

Roger was suddenly seen scuttling across the floor of his room. He emerged at the bathroom door, and in a flash, had disappeared under the chest of drawers. Robin surmised that because he was a big human, Roger was afraid of him. If Robin were a baby, rats in the projects have been known to eat their heads off. What a dismal thought for such a beautiful morning, Robin concluded.

Coffee was perking in the chrome-plated percolator on his dresser. McElroy kept a couple of donuts he bought at a donut shop in his refrigerator. If he left them in the dresser drawer, for sure they'd be destroyed overnight by the infamous Roger. The couple donuts, a glass of orange juice, another product he kept in the refrigerator, and maybe four cups of coffee made up his breakfast that day. He always saved a little coffee in the chrome-plated container for Cynthia when she came in later to visit in the day.

"It's Number One again this week," Jenny Bright announced over the airwaves. "'Flashdance (What a Feeling)', by Irene Cara on WZMX...." This had been the fifth week that song had been Number One, Robin noticed. Although the song had been up there for a while, McElroy still listened to it in its entirety. At its conclusion, the disc-jockey's voice immediately came on again. "That's Irene Cara at Chicago's Big 96. Jenny Bright here with you until ten o'clock. Listen for Rick Zachary and his 'flaming' itinerary of oldies such as "YMCA" by the Village People, "Daniel" by Elton John, and "Killer Queen" by Queen, here exclusively during the afternoon on WZMX.

"Etta McCutcheon is no longer living, but she left behind a legacy which the Etta McCutcheon Bakeries of today still rigidly follow. When Etta McCutcheon opened her business, she used only the best ingredients and strived for perfection in every batch of baked goods. She believed that the public would take notice. And they did! And today, those same superior quality breads, cakes, cookies and pies are still leaving the Etta McCutcheon Bakeries every day.

"Pay a visit to Etta McCutcheon's section of baked goods at your neighborhood Fashley Food Store. When you do, you can be assured of the best ingredients and perfection in every batch. This week at Fashley, there is a special on Etta McCutcheon's Blueberry Coffee Cake. Just a dollar-nineteen, at Fashley.

"WZMX Accuweather. It's going to be a hot one today. Baseball weather. Put on your T-shirts and cutoffs. We're going to have highs of 88 to 90 throughout the city. Presently, I've got 79 at O'Hare, 76 at the Lakefront, and 81 at WZMX. It's rising fast on the Top 40, here's 'Every Breath You Take' by the Police at Chicago's Big 96...."

Robin poured himself a cup of coffee. He also took a bite out of one of his donuts. It was going to be just another hot, boring day in The Windy City.

He lit up a cigarette with his steel lighter, after finishing his donut. Between puffs, he sipped on his steaming hot cup of coffee.

McElroy was wearing his black, cleated boots, a pair of blue jeans and a dark blue cotton T-shirt with the brand name "Rudfunk" scrawled across it in white letters. He decided it would be better in the park than cooped up in this sultry hotel room. His cross necklace was dangling from his neck. The cross figure hung at the center of his chest. Nobody could take that away from him. Nobody. He stood up, walked across the room and opened the door. Robin decided to leave the coffee pot on; Cynthia would be around for some later. Then he left the room.

Robin seated himself at his familiar park bench. It was another weekday in The Windy City. He watched a mother and her two young children having a picnic on a blanket not too far away from him. Pigeons were strutting about the park in search of food morsels and handouts.

After a while, he stood up and started walking along the sidewalk. The Sheiks' vandalism still had not been erased. That building was still under construction at the park's south end. Men wearing brown work outfits and scarlet-colored hard hats toiled the day away.

The jackhammer was reverberating at the site. Blue and white flames tipped the nozzles of welding torches. Riveters were hard at work. When the jackhammer wasn't operating, grating voices of workers could be heard. Often they'd swear at one another. A pile of debris was aflame in the front of the site. Red and yellow flames charred the garbage to a crisp. The heat of this fire rose into the air, forming a sheen that was not totally lucid in the air above it.

Robin then turned his sights the other way, walking back towards the hotel. The sign that read "The Saint James Hotel" came into sight. It was a dingy sign. Its yellow background, with red letters never ceased to intrigue him. Then there were those holes that let through the white light. That sign had never been fixed. Yet that sign endured. No doubt that dingy sign had endured for the past fifty years! Yes. Robin concluded there was indeed a God in every part of the world, no matter how run down and old that part of the world might be.

Chapter Twenty-Five

Robin found himself a new place to eat in a hole-in-the-wall establishment called Sandra's Diner. It was located six blocks from The Saint James Hotel on another appendage from Halsted Street. Sandra's was open twenty-four hours a day and was the epitome of a greasy spoon.

McElroy chowed down on a greasy grilled cheese sandwich late one afternoon during the first week of July. The diner was air-conditioned, and Robin found it to be a pleasant escape from the afternoon heat in Chicago. He had a Coke, coleslaw, and a large slice of dill pickle to go with it. There were also potato chips on his plate. The entire meal at Sandra's cost him only $3.45. Cheap.

When he returned to his hotel room, he put on a fresh pot of coffee. Cynthia had been complaining lately that her coffee wasn't fresh. Robin could live with that. He couldn't live with a "space cadet." The fascination of his not having to work and seeming to have "all that money" had probably worn off as well. McElroy knew she liked him. She was also no dog; there could be other men if she wanted them. Seeing that she came in to visit him almost every single day, without fail, her interest truly appeared to be genuine.

Of late, Robin found himself thinking about Cynthia almost as much as he did about Mary when he was dating her. That was his "way." Was he in love? He didn't know for sure. Time had taken its toll on him; she was often on his mind now. That was the way she had wanted it to be. There weren't too many things about her he didn't like; just a few. But they were major things.

What was he doing in Chicago anyway? The people in Chicago, in general, appeared to be so unfriendly. What was he doing with this "girl" who was five years younger, who looked and acted like a teenager? There were things about him she should know, but would never know. If they were to marry, they'd certainly have to be revealed. The fact that he was a fugitive was one. The fact that he had stolen that money was another. And the fact that his name was not really Robin McElroy was yet another. If all this information was unleashed, how would she react? If she loved him, really loved him, it may not matter. From what he knew about love, he figured she didn't really know a damned thing about love. While all these thoughts were rolling around in Robin's mind, there was a knock at his door.

"Come in," he said. "The door's unlocked."

"Hi," Cynthia said as she entered. She looked around the room a little bit to see that everything was in order. Nothing had changed.

"I see you put on some fresh coffee for me. It's still perking," she told him.
"How was work?"

"The usual. My inconsiderate boss is driving me crazy."

McElroy could tell by the way she was talking that she was not stoned again today. That was appreciated.

"Are we going to Florida this August?" Cynthia inquired again.

"Yes," Robin replied. He'd made up his mind to say "yes" to that so long as he was located in Chicago. By this time was there was no other answer he could give her to that but "yes."

"I'm glad you finally came to your senses about that. It'll do both of us a world of good."

Cynthia poured herself a cup of coffee and sat down on the bed next to Robin. She wanted to put her arm around him, but felt it would be better if she didn't. Why hadn't he promoted anything sexual with her by this time? She wondered about that. It was up to him to promote it, she thought. It seemed as if he was almost abnormal not to have. The most he'd ever promoted with her was holding hands. After three months of friendship, that, to her, was nothing. Maybe he was too much of a gentleman for her?

"Have you seen Roger lately?" she asked.

"I saw him a couple of days ago. He never sticks around long enough for me to get a good look at him."

"It's probably for the better," Cynthia added.

On this particular day, Robin wasn't much in the mood for conversation. He'd been doing a lot of thinking, and his train of thought was beginning to get confused. The end result was that he didn't have much to say.

"Can I use your bathtub?" Cynthia suddenly asked. "Mine's not working."

"Sure. Go ahead." Robin replied.

While she closed the door behind her, turned the water on and began to strip, she was aware of the fact that she had told him a lie. Her bathtub was working fine.

"You should do something about these streaks of rust," she said, calling out from behind the closed door.

"They don't bother me," Robin told her.

She climbed into the tub, and remained silent while she bathed. While she was in the tub, McElroy poured himself a cup of coffee. Then he lit up a cigarette. Time passed. Cynthia was getting up her nerve. Could this make or break their friendship? She wanted it on more intimate terms anyway. She knew he was no virgin. Why did she have to promote this?

"I'm coming out," she finally said.

While the water was rolling down the drain, she opened the door and entered his bedroom in the nude, When Robin looked her way, he saw her standing there with her arms at her side, leaving nothing to the imagination. He looked her over for a moment; this was a side of her he had never seen. There was a smattering of freckles across the tops of her white, well-rounded breasts. The nipples were both tiny and a light hue of pink. Lower down her waist curved inward, then formed the remainder of the "hourglass" at her hips. A curly V-shaped tuft of red pubic hair housed her crotch.

"Get back in there and put your clothes back on," he told her.

"I want you to fuck me."

"The answer is 'no.' Now got back to the bathroom and put your clothes on."

"I'm not a virgin," she protested.

"I could tell that the third time I talked to you," McElroy replied.

She forced some tears into her eyes. Her hair was ruffled up atop her head. She had purposely mussed it up to appear sensuous to him.

"Don't you love me by now?" she asked, taking a sniff with her nose while a teardrop rolled down her left cheek.

"No."

"What's wrong with you? Every other man I've ever dated has wanted to go to bed with me."

"Then you and I went to a different school." This time she really burst into tears. She slammed the bathroom door behind her, crying profusely. She'd failed! She'd failed! She'd failed! If he didn't love her by now, he was never going to. That's what Miss Craig was thinking at this time. Why had she wasted all this time on him? She was only going to end up having hurt herself. Again.

McElroy was in a stupor. Her body had been enticing. Naturally. But it was her. It was her he couldn't deal with. She wanted to marry him. She must've thought that sex was her ticket for a wedding ring. He wanted her out of his apartment right away. He could never marry her!

"I don't know why I ever became your friend!" she wailed as she stomped out of the bathroom with her clothes on. "You are such a bastard!"

At that, she disappeared out the bedroom door.

Chapter Twenty-Six

It was 8:30 in the morning four days after the incident with Cynthia. She had not come to visit him since. Did he love her? He asked himself that question. He'd been in love before. The answer was finally "no."

The couple next door, in the room opposite Cynthia's, was having another one of their tooth-and-nail senseless arguments. Robin decided he wasn't going to miss those two. He'd never even met them in person and he already hated them.

On this particular day, his radio was not playing.

The fan in his room was whirring. The heat in the city had escalated even more of late. On this day, he wanted to hear no Chicago music, weather reports, news, or commercials. He was sick and tired of living in this place.

He put on his blue jeans, black-cleated boots, and "Rudfunk" T-shirt, then closed the bedroom door behind him and walked the six blocks to Sandra's Diner. On the way, he could see people along the sidewalk clad in tank tops, halter tops, T-shirts, "fruity-Colored" Hawaiian shirts, cut-offs, shorts, and light cotton dresses and other light apparel in hues of white, yellow, turquoise and lavender. It was summer in the city. And Robin McElroy did not fit in with the mainstream of things. He strolled down the walk in his "off-color" blue jeans and T-shirt, sporting that gold emblem which signified that God was within him.

Did he really need anybody else anyways?

The diner was a beige-colored stone affair with long rectangular windows around all sides and had a black shingled roof that sloped on a forty-degree angle. Inside there were old wooden chairs surrounding wooden tables and a white Formica counter with myriads of silver-colored cabinets and machinery in the background. The setup had to rate as nothing less than "tacky."

At the Formica counter, Robin ordered a bowl of whole wheat cereal, a glass of orange juice, a cup of coffee, and had a couple of slices of toast with jelly on the side. He ate his breakfast slowly. He enjoyed being within this air-conditioning. Once he left the restaurant, it was back to "hell's pits" with no way of evading it. Over the radio at Sandra's, he heard that the temperature was going to be ninety-five degrees on this day.

After finishing his breakfast, Robin took a walk out to Manteno Park. He sat on his old, familiar green park bench while the heat gradually rose in the city. He figured it had to be at least 85 or 90 degrees already. The heat was beginning to overwhelm him. There was no place to escape it for any length of time.

Two black women, middle-aged, sauntered past him on the sidewalk while he was seated at the green bench. He heard one of the ladies say to the other, "That man's a saint."

He watched them continue down the sidewalk, cross the street the hotel was on, then disappear into The Saint James Hotel. In other words, talk about this strange man was beginning to go around. They knew him now. They just didn't want to "venture" him. Of late he realized he had been getting known in this area. Robin surmised that was yet another good reason to leave town.

Everything was the usual, north and south of the park. The building south of the park was still under construction while the men in their scarlet-colored helmets labored in troughs of "hell's fire." The Saint James Hotel sign still radiated its light from the North. And here Robin sat on his green park bench with the sidewalk, "the avenue of life," paved through the green grass in front of him. It's disfiguring graffiti was scrawled across the "avenue of life" in the light of the sun.

McElroy lit up a cigarette and puffed on it while he suffered in the unbearable summer heat. What should he tell Cynthia before he was to leave? Should he tell her anything? Should he just go and forget that he ever met her? This looked as if it were going to be another day where his train of thought was scrambled. The unavoidable heat made the process of practical thinking very difficult. He held the cross figure on his necklace between his thumb and forefinger. Nobody could take that away from him. Nobody.

He decided he could cool off a little if he filled his bathtub with cold water and sat in it. Robin snuffed out his cigarette on the sidewalk in the park with his boot, then returned to his hotel room.

Past the old wooden door which served as the entrance to The Saint James Hotel, there was almost total darkness. A light could be seen through the caged window to the desk clerk's quarters. The scar-faced desk clerk nodded at Robin when he entered. The heat in the enclosed staircase was overwhelming. It must've been at least 90 degrees in there! Beads of sweat had formed on his forehead and sweat was dripping down his face. His breathing in this heat was congested.

When he entered his room, he immediately turned on the cold-water handle on the bathtub and began to strip. He added a little hot water from the hot water handle because the cold water coming out of the other faucet was icy cold. It must be a deep well, he thought.

He immersed himself in that bathwater for hours.

Robin smoked cigarette after cigarette. The fan in his bedroom was whirring at full speed. The temperature in the city continued to escalate. He began to wonder if all this heat wasn't going to make him sick. Finally. He fell asleep in the bathtub.

Later that afternoon, he decided he must really leave this city today. He packed his suitcase in a torpid manner and noticed the continuous heat was making him sick. Robin lay on his bed. His stomach was queasy. He rushed to the toilet and vomited. When he returned to his bed, his head was still swimming. He decided he'd wait until Cynthia returned home from work that day, then he'd tell her he was leaving town. He wanted to be fair about the whole thing. As fair as he could be about it.

Later, there was a light knock at his door.

"The door's open," he called out.

Cynthia opened it.

"Hi," she said, meekly. Neither one of them had forgotten what had happened the other day.

"I'm sick," Robin said. "I've got the flu or something."

"It's probably the heat," she told him. She seated herself by him on his bed. She put her hand on his forehead. "You do have a fever," she added.

Should he tell her he was leaving town today? He thought about that, suddenly. He felt that if he stuck around here any longer, he was going to die.

How was she going to react to his leaving? He thought about that too. There would probably be a protest. He knew there would be a protest. She would try to keep him cooped up here as long as she could. He decided that instant that he was not going to tell her he was leaving town that day. He knew the way he was at this point in time, he couldn't fight her. His eyes became closed.

"I can see you don't feel like talking today," she told him. "If you need anything, I'm right next door."

"Thanks," Robin mumbled.

At that, she stood up and walked out the door. The thought of her caring about him like she did bothered Robin. Didn't she say something about "love" the last time he saw her? Oh no! He had to get a "divorce" from this community. He could never marry her, and she had fallen in love with him! Hadn't she? He was sorry! No. He did not love her. It was strictly "one-sided." He started to feel sorry for her. She had made the mistake of putting all her eggs in one basket, and as the fable goes, the basket of eggs fell off her head. If she loved him, which it seemed apparent now she did, for sure she was going to miss him and be hurt by his leaving.

Chapter Twenty-Seven

Early that same evening, a cold front moved in off the lake; there was a twenty-degree drop in temperature and thundershowers. The beating of the rain outside his open window woke him up. When that cool breeze circulated through his bedroom, Robin felt as if God had answered a prayer for him. He lay awake on his bed for an hour.

Suddenly, he heard a knock at Cynthia's door. He knew it wasn't his door. The rapping sound was too distant. McElroy decided to investigate to see who it was. If it was Rat and Ike, they were in trouble! He opened his bedroom door and peered into the hallway. It was, indeed, the "dope-dealing duo."

Robin's mind began racing. He spasmodically reached for the chrome-plated coffee pot on his dresser. The container was empty. While Rat and Ike disappeared in through Cynthia's doorway, Robin scrambled in the door after them. Ike was first to spin around and take notice of the oncoming attacker. While his eyes bulged in disbelief, the coffee pot came crashing down upon his forehead, creating a dull "thud." It put a dent in the side of the chrome pot. Ike dropped like a leaf to the floor of her hotel room, unconscious and with a concussion.

"No!" Cynthia screamed. She could not believe what Robin had just done. McElroy closed the door behind him. Rat drew his switchblade from his pocket.

"I'm going to kill you," Rat whispered. He pushed the button on his switchblade, and it clicked open.

"Stop!" Cynthia shrieked.

Robin removed his switchblade from his pocket and flicked open the blade. "I have one of those too," he warned.

Cynthia was now speechless. She put her hands over her face. He was doing this for her, wasn't he? The cross dangled below Robin's chest as he hunched himself in a stance for an attack.

"Don't," Cynthia pleaded in a murmur through her hands.

There was venom in the eyes of both of the men. There was a long period of silence, then Rat lashed out at Robin with his knife. He missed!

"You don't even know how to use that thing," Rat told him, watching Robin with his switchblade. "I'm going to split your gut!"

Cynthia was now kneeling down on the floor. She had her hands over her face. She couldn't watch. She simply couldn't bear it. This whole fight was on account of her.

Rat lashed out at Robin again and Robin dodged his cut at him. Rat pointed his knife his way, gradually forcing McElroy into a corner.

"You're a dead man," Rat said.

Robin's eyes darted back and forth desperately. He knew he was being cornered, and he was suddenly starting to realize there was no way out. Cynthia was still kneeling on the floor, not watching. Rat eased in slowly, his knife extended, anticipating any move Robin might make in his defense.

Both men were beginning to perspire under the arms. This was tough, dirty work. Rat never discontinued his train of concentration. At seemingly the last moment of his life, Robin quickly discovered a way out. That chair! That chair that was not included with his room, but with hers! It was a wooden rocking chair. Rat's concentration on lunging for the kill was never broken. Robin grasped that rocking chair, spun slightly to evade his strike with the knife, and struck him across the hands with it! Robin still held on to his switchblade. Rat's switchblade clacked onto the floor upon impact of the chair. Robin dropped the chair, maintaining his grip on the handle of his switchblade. While Rat was reaching for his knife on the floorboards, Robin lunged at him with all his might and thrust the blade of his knife as far as he could into Rat's left thigh. The tip of his blade ended up going entirely through his leg! Rat's eyes bulged in terror while he saw the handle of Robin's switchblade protruding from the side of his leg! His mouth became agape, and he let out a bloodcurdling scream! Blood was gushing from the incision, streaming rapidly down his pants. A pool of blood began to form on the floorboards near his shoe while he let out another hair-raising scream! A sudden fear of Robin became instilled within him. Rat hobbled across the floor of the bedroom, leaving a trail of blood in his wake.

Cynthia had taken her hands away from her face and also let out a scream when she saw the switchblade stuck in Rat's leg and the blood pouring out of the wound. Rat hobbled and limped to the door, opened it, then flailed his painfully injured leg as fast as he could to the staircase. He hopped down the staircase on his right leg, tripped, tumbled, and screamed again when he reached the bottom of the stairs via the fall.

Cynthia was crying in her room now. She was still down on her knees. Robin felt so sorry for her. He stood above her, giving her the option of clinging to his leg. This was all too much for her to handle. While she sobbed over the violent incident which had just occurred in her hotel room, Robin withdrew his most prized possession from around his neck, then placed it over her head and around her neck.

"Keep this," He whispered gently.

The cross necklace hung around her neck now. He had just parted with something that was a part of him.

It was an item he placed more value on than anything else he'd ever owned. And he had just given it to her. "I must leave town," he told her suddenly. He had just found the perfect reason for a fast exit into another community. He was leaving for a reason now that she had to understand. It was not within his jurisdiction to take the action he had taken against these men. They both knew it.

"I know," Cynthia replied. "Get out of here!"

Robin rushed to his room, grabbed his large suitcase, his small suitcase, and his radio; then he dashed out the fire escape on the far end of the corridor opposite the staircase. Neither the desk clerk nor Cynthia ever saw him again.

Chapter Twenty-Eight

On Halsted Street, Robin flagged down a checker cab and rode in it to a bus depot in The Loop. It was still raining outdoors. While the windshield wipers on the olive-drab-colored cab slapped away the pouring rain, Robin remained silent and nervous in the back seat. Streetlights loomed, glowing in the darkness along Halsted Street with a hazy sheen surrounding them in the precipitation-laden night air. While riding in that charcoal-colored back seat of the checker cab, a mirage of Cynthia's countenance appeared in his mind. He could see her weeping on the floor of her hotel room with his cross necklace suspended around her neck. There was a vacancy where that cross necklace used to hang around his neck now. He had sacrificed a part of himself in an act of God that he hoped would benefit her. It was God who had told him to drape that prized possession around her neck. Something good should come from what he had done, seeing that the value of his gift was nothing less than "priceless." His mind's eye once again focused upon her crying in her bedroom. In retrospect, Robin must've looked to her like a nightcrawler to a hungry bluegill. Unfortunately, he had to remove his hook from the water before she could devour it. When he arrived at the depot, he tipped the cabbie five dollars and hoped the police weren't already looking for him.

At the depot, he scanned the departures table for any city a bus was leaving to soon. In the white background with black letters, he came upon a bus leaving for Montgomery, Alabama, in half an hour. It was rather cool in the bus depot at this hour of the night; it was air-conditioned but the air-conditioning had been shut off. Outdoors it was now a cool sixty-five degrees.

Having forgotten about the insufferable heat he'd experienced that day, he reckoned Montgomery, Alabama, was as good a destination as any. He was going to be sure, next time, the residence he took up down there was air-conditioned. The bus would be air-conditioned. It would not be that bad. He entered the line to the ticket booth, then purchased a ticket one-way to Montgomery at the ticket window, then found himself a seat on a long, dark brown wooden bench in the depot. Nervously, he chain-smoked in the lobby of the bus depot. He bought a newspaper to bury his face in while he sat on that bench. He tapped his foot constantly while he waited for the announcement that his bus was ready. After fifteen minutes, there was an announcement that the bus bound for Montgomery had arrived. People were asked to board it.

His large suitcase was stored in the trunk compartment underneath the passenger area of the bus. His small suitcase and the radio remained with him. Robin gave his ticket to the bus driver. He took a seat on the "starboard" side of the bus next to a window, then gazed out the window watching the people in the terminal. The bus ended up being five minutes late in leaving.

A policeman caught his eye while the bus started to move. The cop was looking at the bus, but he didn't make any motion to the bus driver to stop it. Apparently, the suspect in the Rat and Ike attack had not been traced to this location, but he was certain the police were now in search of a Robin McElroy.

Robin glanced at his wristwatch. The time was 9:20. As the bus exited the depot and started through the streets of Chicago, McElroy let out a sigh of relief. Nobody was sitting next to him at this time. He removed his driver's license from his wallet, then brought out his cigarette lighter and set the plastic-coated identification piece aflame. He made sure nobody was watching him. A yellow flame licked up his driver's license while the plastic cover bubbled under in the heat of it. The identification card turned to black. He stamped out the charred remains on the floor below his feet. He lit up a cigarette, then, and relaxed as best he could. His name was Rodney Applegate now. He had to remember that.

The drone of the engine could be heard while the bus automatically shifted through its gears. The bus passed under a long row of streetlights which illuminated the interior of the vehicle. There were not too many people on the bus. Rodney preoccupied himself with his newspaper under a light which he had switched on above him. He read the sports section. Then the comics. He was still nervous. He lit up another cigarette.

While the bus was traveling along the expressway, he switched on his portable radio. It was still tuned to his favorite WZMX. "Never Gonna Let You Go," by Sergio Mendez, was playing when he first turned it on. It was a contemporary hit that had entered the Top 40 in May.

Rodney Applegate was quite familiar with it by now. Before the song ended, he turned it off again. He was too nervous to listen. He had never done anything before like he'd done that night. He could still see Rat screaming after having been stuck like a pig. Would the cops ever find him? At this point, did he really care? Maybe he was better off in jail? His life was trash at this point in time anyway.

Rain was beating gently against his window now. The huge windshield wipers on the bus were slapping away. Rodney peered out the front window of the bus. There were the red taillights of cars, not too many cars, to be seen ahead of him. The bus was now traveling at a hefty fifty-five miles per hour. He wanted to go to sleep and forget about what he had done, but he couldn't. The recollection of what he had done that night continued to gnaw away at him.

Gradually, the lights of the city thinned out. He stared out the side window of the bus, watching the cars pass by below him. The raindrops gently sprinkled upon his window. He lit up another cigarette. The thought of getting some sleep was still heavy on his mind, but after all this excitement, he couldn't. He soon heard the reverberating bus engine start to wind down. The bus was slowing down for a toll booth.

Rodney looked up to the sky. The stars were easier to see now that they were out of the heart of the city. The sky was clearer. There was a noticeable difference. He was beginning to feel emancipated. This was the first time he had been outside of Chicago since March. He turned off the reading light above him and closed his eyes. The darkness now surrounding him helped. The bus was rolling at fifty-five miles per hour. again down the toll way.

He thought about that cross he'd given to Cynthia. Rodney felt as if he had had to. She deserved it, and whatever good came from it as a result of his handing it down to her. Nobody could take that cross from him, but it didn't mean he couldn't give it away to someone very special. Did he love her? Again. The answer was still "no." And the answer would always be "no." She sure gave it a whirl. He had to hand it to her. He must've been someone awfully special to her. Cynthia must've felt shattered by this time. By now Rodney figured she was probably sitting in the police station having to answer all kinds of questions. What was going to be her fate? His fate? What were the police going to do about Rat and Ike? He hoped he'd never have to return to Chicago to find out. While Rodney was thinking about all this, he drifted off into slumber.

Chapter Twenty-Nine

When he awoke, the sun was shining. He immediately glanced at his wristwatch. The time was 10:40 in the morning. Mental exhaustion. It had been mental exhaustion that had made him sleep so many hours. His mind had tied itself up in a knot with worry the night before. Where was he? The bus was traveling down a downgrade. By now he must've reached a portion of the Appalachian Mountain Chain. Where was he? Alarums of tall trees and blades of green grass could be seen through "portside" and "starboard" side windows. The terrain was uneven, hilly.

He turned on the radio with hopes of finding out just where he was. When he switched it on, all he got was static. He turned the tuning dial until he reached a clear band of reception. Rodney found himself lackadaisically listening to a commercial for Winn Dixie Supermarkets. Yes. Indeed, he was south of the Mason-Dixon Line now. The towering sign from the interstate to the right of him advertised the presence of a Chevron Gas Station. There were none of those in The Windy City. A blue sign to the right of him announced that he was traveling on 1-65 South. A green sign above the road in white letters at an exit read "Birmingham" (with a white arrow below it). He knew, then, that he was already south of Nashville, Tennessee. He had traveled this road before.

There was no rain going on in this part of the country. As a matter of fact, it looked hot out in the boondocks. The air-conditioner was on in the bus. It was most likely a sweltering summer day in Dixieland.

A woman in her twenties was seated next to him on the bus now. She was reading a magazine. *Cosmopolitan.* She had kinky, long blond hair, bright red lips, blue eyes with no mascara, and an aquiline nose. She was pretty. Should he promote a conversation with her? No. He had been sleeping when she arrived in the seat next to him.

While the minutes ticked past, Rodney felt a sudden craving for a cigarette. His nicotine buzzer had gone on. After sticking a cigarette between his lips and igniting it with his steel lighter, the woman asked, "Can I have a cigarette? I forgot to buy a pack in Nashville." Her voice carried a Southern accent. It sounded pleasant to Rodney Applegate.

"They're light," Rodney warned.

"Just so long as they're not menthol," she replied.

"Do you live in Nashville?" Rodney asked.

"Yes."

"Where are you headed?"

"Montgomery. That's the next and last stop," she told him, as if he should've already known that.

"What's in Montgomery?" Rodney asked.

The young woman stuck one of Applegate's cigarettes between her cardinal-colored lips and began fumbling through her purse for a book of matches. Applegate immediately obliged her with his lighter. He struck a flame to the tip of her smoke, and she inhaled.

"Thank you," she mumbled. "My mother."

The bus continued traveling along the uneven terrain on 1-65 headed South. The conversation between the two of them tacitly died right there. Rodney's radio was still playing. The song "Sweet Home Alabama," by Lynyrd Skynyrd, was on the air. One minute later, a sign on the right side of the interstate read: WELCOME TO ALABAMA.

Epilogue

(One Year Later)

Rodney Applegate, after arriving in Montgomery the year before, decided to buy a small, dark brown wooden shack off of Route #231 west of Dothan, Alabama. The cabin had been abandoned for a while before he purchased it and was in desperate need of some work. He fixed it up himself. The price was extremely moderate, and with an air-conditioner whirring outside of the shack, he found himself able to tolerate the immense summer Southern heat. There were no other houses within half a mile of him. He was on his own. Now he felt nearer to God than ever before.

That suitcase full of Ulysses S. Grant denominations, well, he kept that safely tucked away in a chest of drawers. He would often go two or three weeks without seeing a soul. God was always with him, though. He liked this part of the country far better than Chicago. The Windy City. The Hog Butcher. He'd finally found peace of mind.

There was a stone fireplace in this ramshackle living unit. This was his only source of heat when the mercury took a nosedive into the '40s and '50s during the winter months in southern Alabama.

He bought a fifteen-year-old jeep that had developed an uncommon, terminal case of rust in this Southern state. It had been owned by a man who lived on the Florida Panhandle near the Gulf of Mexico. No doubt the saltwater Gulf air had its influence upon the body condition of the vehicle. It was obtained for a minimal $825, and for some reason kicked over every time he turned the ignition switch. It was dependable transportation for the few times he used it. If the "heat" from the Federal Government ever got too hot again, he reckoned he'd climb behind the wheel of his jeep and maybe make a mad dash into Texas or Mexico. He hoped, after having invested about one-quarter of his suitcase loaded with Ulysses S. Grant denominations into his shack, that he would never have to make that move. He was hoping that this time he'd lost himself for good.

Rodney often wondered whatever became of Cynthia. He would never know. His unpleasant past with people had finally ended.

Cynthia, shaken up by what had happened to Rat and Ike, and knowing how strongly the man she loved felt about her cocaine addiction, went on to get drug-rehabilitation after Rat and Ike went to jail. Yes. The two of them were sentenced to ten years for dealing cocaine.

By the summer of '84, Cynthia was back on the track in the work world. She'd found a new job, this one in The Chicago Loop. At the same time, she upmoded her living conditions. The Saint James Hotel was no longer her home. She was able to upmode, too, because she was no longer "paying through the nose" for cocaine. There was also a guy in her new place of work, at this point in time, who had taken a real interest in her. She decided to play it "cool" with him; she had not forgotten how much it had hurt to lose Robin McElroy. Cynthia wore that cross necklace Robin gave her to work every day. Somehow, during the turmoil and heat of that hellish night in July of '83, when he placed that cross around her neck, Cynthia Craig too had discovered a friend in God. God went to work on upgrading her life immediately.

In the light yellow cafeteria of her new workplace, Cynthia and her new boyfriend were eating their lunch. Cynthia was having a reuben sandwich, milk, and tossed salad. Travis Archibald, which was the name of her new "bright-eyed and bushy-tailed" boyfriend, sat across the table from her tending to his cheeseburger, french fries, ketchup, and milk carton. He had stylishly close-cropped black hair, a lantern jaw, bright white teeth in a sunny smile which flashed often, and bushy black eyebrows. He was handsome. He looked upon the cross necklace Cynthia was wearing. She had never spoken a word to him about Robin McElroy and promised herself she never would. There had been a "hole" left in heart which would probably never mend. She did not want to make herself vulnerable by talking about him. She would never forget him.

"Where did you get the cross necklace?" Travis asked her.

There was a long moment of hesitation. Miss Craig rolled her eyes away evasively then returned her glance to once again face him.

"The best friend I ever had gave it to me once. Can we leave it at that?"